NIGHTMARE HALL

THE SILENT SCREAM
THE ROOMMATE
DEADLY ATTRACTION
THE WISH
THE SCREAM TEAM
GUILTY
PRETTY PLEASE
THE EXPERIMENT
THE NIGHT WALKER
SORORITY SISTER

Last Date

"Call me."

"Hello?" said Demi.

"Why didn't you call me?" asked the voice at the other end of the phone.

"Who is this?" asked Demi.

"You had your chance," the voice intoned.

"Who *are* you?"

"Your dream date. Don't you know who I am?"

"I don't have to listen to this!" Demi said.

But the voice went on. "You had your chance. Now you have to pay."

The room spun. Everything in it seemed to be moving. To have a life of its own.

Demi realized she was holding something in her hand. The *Chronicle*. With her picture on the front page. Why? What was happening?

Then she saw the headline: KILLER DATE.

Terrifying thrillers by Diane Hoh:

Funhouse

The Accident

The Invitation

The Train

The Fever

Nightmare Hall: The Silent Scream

Nightmare Hall: The Roommate

Nightmare Hall: Deadly Attraction

Nightmare Hall: The Wish

Nightmare Hall: The Scream Team

Nightmare Hall: Guilty

Nightmare Hall: Pretty Please

Nightmare Hall: The Experiment

Nightmare Hall: The Night Walker

Nightmare Hall: Sorority Sister

Nightmare Hall: Last Date

NIGHTMARE HALL

Last Date

DIANE HOH

SCHOLASTIC INC.
New York Toronto London Auckland Sydney

No part of this publication may be reproduced in whole or in part, or stored in a retrieval system, or transmitted in any form or by any means, electronic, mechanical, photocopying, recording, or otherwise, without written permission of the publisher. For information regarding permission, write to Scholastic Inc., 555 Broadway, New York, NY 10012.

ISBN 0-590-48133-9

12 11 10 9 8 7 6 5 4 3 2 1   4 5 6 7 8 9/9

Printed in the U.S.A.   01

First Scholastic printing, May 1994

Prologue

Call me.

Oh yes. Yes. She was used to telling people what to do. Used to getting what she wanted.

Used to having it all.

Call me.

To her, it was just a game. Her game. Her rules.

But the rules had just changed. And *she* was about to find out.

It wasn't a game anymore. Not a dating game.

Now it was the dying game.

Could she play by the rules of the dying game?

No.

Probably not.

But she would have a chance. A chance to prove herself worthy.

Pity death always won in the end. . . .

Chapter 1

"You can't do that!"

"I can't?" Demi Blake raised one eyebrow. "Why not?"

Shannon Thompson gave a little gasp of shocked laughter. "Because . . . because . . . because anything could happen!"

"That's just it." Demi rolled over on her stomach, pushed her shades up on her nose, and smoothed the piece of newspaper in her hand. "I *want* something to happen. I'm bored."

Sprawled on the grass of the Salem University Commons, the two girls were soaking up the last bit of sun on an unseasonably warm spring afternoon. The campus, for that one golden day, had fallen into a summer rhythm and most of the students were taking an impromptu holiday, reading, playing Frisbee, sunbathing in every square inch of light.

Demi wasn't sunbathing. She was wearing black bicycle shorts, a sleek black skin-fitting long-sleeved top and dark glasses. With her pale red-gold hair and translucent white skin, Demi didn't do sun. But she basked in the warmth like a dangerous golden cat with strange green eyes.

By contrast, her best friend, Shannon, looked like an all-American student. In her white halter top, pink baggy shorts, pink headband holding short dark curls off her round, dimpled face, she was a parent's dream of a perfect daughter.

No two people could have been more different. Shannon radiated energy and indiscriminate laughter, while Demi seemed a study in stillness, in wary, bored observation.

Until she moved.

She moved now, sitting up with startling speed and grace to snare the campus paper, which was threatening to come undone in the breeze and scatter across the grass.

"I'm bored," Demi repeated in her soft, throaty voice. She flipped the paper back open and ran her finger down one of the columns in the advertising section.

"CALL ME." The words were blazoned across the top of the section. Below, a small blurb said:

4

Welcome to Salem's newest game — the dating game. Send your ad to our personal column and find a good time, a new scene — or maybe even true love. The people who answer the ads can phone a message to our special "CALL ME" number. Each advertiser will have a private code to pick up his or her messages only. You can choose to return the calls you want.

Below it was the CALL ME number. And below that was the new student personal column.

"Listen to this." Demi read aloud: *"Pretty woman, I'm yours. I like football, parties, and serious fun. CALL ME.* That doesn't sound too bad."

Shannon pointed. "Yeah, but look at this one: *"Handsome guy seeks gorgeous girl to make the perfect couple, especially if you like independent film festivals and sushi."* She made a face. "Ugh. Raw fish."

"I'm going to do it."

Shannon's brown eyes widened. "You're not! You don't even like sushi!"

"Shannon, hello? Of course I'm not going to

answer an ad. I'm going to place one."

"For a date?" Shannon's eyes widened. "You're not really *serious*."

"I've never been more serious in my life." Demi smiled wickedly. "I'm going to place an ad of my own."

"Demi!" Shannon shrieked so loudly that students lolling in the grass nearby glanced over curiously. Blushing, Shannon lowered her voice. "Demi! You can't! What if, what if . . . what if some psycho calls you?"

"Girl, you have a *vivid* imagination. But I promise, if a psycho calls, I won't call him back. Okay?"

"How could you tell he was a psycho? Psychos can be very charming. Very clever. Devious."

"Hmmm." Demi's expression grew thoughtful. "Then maybe I *will* call him back."

"It's not something to joke about, Demi! You're not really going to do this, right? I mean, you wouldn't really dare do something like that, putting an ad in the stupid personal column? Uncool max. Puh-leeze."

"I don't agree. I think it's a great idea. The whole column, I mean. When I joined the *Chronicle*, I thought it was kind of dull. But this makes it hugely more interesting. In fact, you know what? Answering some of these ads, or putting one in would make a great feature story!" Some of the boredom left Demi's voice.

"But you wouldn't really do it," Shannon insisted. "Not really."

"I would, too."

"Would not."

"I would!"

"I dare you," Shannon shot back. "I dare you, Demi Blake."

For a long moment the two girls stared at each other. Then Demi smiled, stretched, and began to stand up.

"Where are you going?"

Demi looked down at Shannon. "To the *Chronicle* office to place an ad, where else?"

Shannon shrieked again, but Demi didn't even look back as she sauntered away across the Commons.

Leaning against the doorjamb of the *Chronicle* office, Demi surveyed the room. The only person she saw was Kevin Bork, the managing editor, his head bent over a printout.

It figured, thought Demi. She'd known the moment she met Kevin that he was the serious, intense type, the sort of person who would choose to spend a perfect spring afternoon indoors.

At least the windows were open, though.

That was a point in his favor, she decided. That, and a nice bod and the fact that it was Kevin, surprisingly, who had thought of the idea for CALL ME. Hmm. Hidden depths, maybe?

Her shadow fell across the printout.

Kevin looked up.

For a moment, he didn't seem to focus. Then a broad smile broke across his face.

"Demi! Hi. What are you doing here?"

"What are *you* doing here?" she asked him, sitting on the edge of the desk and swinging her legs.

He looked down and looked back up at her, a faint blush tinging his cheeks.

"Working."

Demi leaned forward. "Me, too."

"You are? On what?"

Demi smiled and let the question linger in the air for a moment, watching Kevin's blush deepen. Then she said, "I had an idea for an article. Something to go with your really great idea for CALL ME."

"Really? You liked my idea?" Some of Kevin's shyness melted away as he smiled eagerly. "Yeah, you know, it was tough convincing the other editors to vote it in. But we've already had a great response in just one week."

"I'm not surprised." Abruptly, Demi abandoned her pose and let her own eagerness show. "But I was thinking, what if someone ran an ad in the personals and then did a piece for the paper on it? You know, about what it was like to meet people, to have dates that way."

Kevin nodded slowly. "I like it. Yeah, I like that a lot. Is it — is it something you want to do?"

"That's the idea," said Demi.

"Really? Cool! You know, it'd be great. Because even the people who hate the whole concept would want to read about it. If it was good stuff, I mean."

"Oh, it'll be good stuff," said Demi.

Kevin smiled up at her and held her gaze for a moment. "You think so?" he answered softly.

Definitely hidden depths, thought Demi.

"I do. Although I don't think it'll be as good as my friend Shannon seems to think it will be."

"What do you mean?" asked Kevin.

"Shannon thinks it's a sure way to meet the weirdos of the world. In her mind, CALL ME is really sort of a 'How to Date Your Local Psycho.' "

"Like in that movie, *Sea of Love*," supplied Kevin. He threw back his head and laughed loudly. "That *would* be a great story! You think you could pull it off?"

"I wish," said Demi. "But I don't think so. I mean, that whole thing about the girl who died at Nightmare Hall, that's one thing, but . . ."

Kevin looked suddenly serious. "Nightingale Hall," he said softly. "They say it's haunted, you know."

The two were quiet for a moment, remembering the awful events that earned the off-campus dorm its nickname, the girl they'd found hanging in her room there. Then, abruptly, Kevin said, "Well, that's another story. So . . ."

"So, let's figure out an ad for CALL ME. A really *good* ad," said Demi. "Something hot."

"Not afraid of weirdos?" asked Kevin, beginning to punch in the code for the personals column on his computer.

Demi laughed. "What's to be afraid of? What, Kevin, I ask you, *what* could possibly go wrong?"

Chapter 2

I'm that kind of girl. Are you my
kind of guy? Let's make a date
for a night you'll never forget.
Call me.

"That's you?" gasped Shannon. She and
Demi were hanging out with some friends in
Gigi LeFarge's room. "Look, guys, this is
Demi's ad. I don't believe you did it! I just don't
believe it."

"You owe me, Shannon," said Demi. "I won
the dare."

"It was a dare? Cool, Demi," said Lacey
Sakurada. "So, who wants some popcorn? And
who's hogging the remote?"

"*C'est moi*," said Gigi LeFarge. "And I am
not giving it up."

"Not even for popcorn?" asked Lacey.

"Then change the channel," Gigi's roommate

Alice complained. "This is the stupidest horror movie I've ever seen."

"I like it," said Gigi calmly. She was French and had a fascination with what she called "American culture," which she insisted she was following by keeping the television in her room on constantly.

"Have you ever seen a horror movie that wasn't stupid?" asked Demi. "I mean, the girl always goes into the woods where the maniac's lurking, after he's killed about a million other people who just happened to have wandered off into the same woods."

"Let's watch reruns," said Alice.

"*The Brady Bunch!*" exclaimed Shannon. "Is it on?"

"Not *The Brady Bunch*, no," said Gigi. "Them I do not like. Demi. Have you taken phone calls for your advertisement yet?"

Demi smiled. "I have."

"Demi! You didn't tell me that!" Shannon looked hurt, but Demi ignored it. Good grief, she wasn't going to tell Shannon *everything*. Demi had barely stopped Shannon in the nick of time when Shannon had started telling about the article Demi was writing for the paper on the dating column thing. *That* would have ruined everything. No one would answer the CALL ME ad if word got out that she was doing a piece on the whole scene.

And she wanted this story to work.

Demi went on. "In fact, I've already set up my first date. This Friday."

"Ah," said Gigi. She sat up, pointed the remote and turned the volume up to shriek.

Immediately someone in the next room began pounding on the wall. "Hey!" a voice called. "I'm trying to study!"

"Bah," said Gigi, turning the sound back down. "You know, I like Salem, but how did I become surrounded by all these people who *study*?"

Gigi looked surprised when everybody laughed. Then she shrugged and turned to Demi. "This date?"

"Yeah," said Shannon.

"Well, his name is Lance . . . and we're going to see a French film."

Shannon made a face. "A French film?"

"What is wrong with a French film?" inquired Gigi.

"Nothing," said Shannon quickly. "It's just that I don't understand them."

"Well, it'll probably have subtitles," Demi continued. "I don't remember what it is called."

"The only French word I know is 'croissant,'" Shannon said.

"It is a good word," Gigi assured her.

"He *is* a French major," Demi reminded them. "He probably knows a few more."

"You better hope so," said Shannon.

"Listen, it's just a date," said Demi. "I'm not going to marry the guy. I'm not going to spend the rest of my life with him."

"*Oui.*" Gigi rolled her eyes. "Unless of course, you die of boredom on this date."

"True," said Demi. "But I don't think this date is going to be such a killer. Hey, who knows? Maybe it'll even be fun."

"I don't believe you're doing this!"

"Have you been talking to Shannon, Jack? There's, like, an echo in here, you know?" Demi pushed back her cup of coffee and looked around Mort par Chocolat for the waiter. Of course, he was nowhere around.

She looked back at the tall, handsome blond guy sitting across from her, who was returning her coaxing smile with a scowl. He was *so* good-looking. Why couldn't she be interested in him anymore?

"Demi, you don't need to get a date through some dweeb personal column in the *Chronicle*. I mean, what am I? Dog food?"

"No." Demi kept the smile on her face with an effort.

Jack kept scowling. "You have a funny way of getting your thrills."

"I'm not trying to be funny . . . look, Jack, we agreed to see other people, right? Am I complaining to you about how you spend your free time or who you spend it with?"

"I'm not trolling for psychos and lunatics in the school paper. Besides, it's like announcing to the world that you'd do anything to date anyone but me! Why don't you just write your name and phone number in all the telephone booths in town?"

"It's not like that!" Where was that waiter? It was coming back to her now — how over-protective Jack was. How possessive. That was why she'd suggested they see other people.

"What's it like then? Suppose you explain it to me."

"It's a dare. I did it on a dare from Shannon, okay? And I don't have to explain anything to you!" Jumping up, Demi dug a handful of money out of her pocket and flung it on the table. "I don't owe you any explanation at all!"

With unexpected swiftness, Jack's hand shot out and clamped down on her wrist. He pulled her toward him.

"Jack! Let go! People are staring!"

His grip tightened.

"Jack! You're hurting me!"

He opened his hand and she jerked free.

"Did you enjoy that? Hurting me? *You're* the one who has a funny way of getting your thrills!"

"Hey! Lose the attitude, Demi, okay? I'm upset. And concerned," answered Jack. "And with good reason."

"Well, forget it," said Demi, "You don't have a right to be upset. And you can take your concern and, and . . . oh, good-bye!" She turned and stalked out of the coffee house, her head high, her cheeks flaming with rage and embarrassment.

She didn't look back to see if everyone who had been watching the fight was watching her leave. She didn't look back to see who the witnesses had been.

She didn't look back to see Jack staring after her, his hands clenched into white-knuckled fists.

And she didn't hear him say, softly, softly to himself, "Better be careful, little girl.

"Or you'll be sorry."

Chapter 3

"Me, I hate blind dates," said Gigi. She was sprawled across the bed in Demi's room and Shannon was sitting on the floor, while Demi was getting ready for her first date from the CALL ME ad.

Demi smiled. "Hey, I've had some real loser dates with people I know. In fact, after Phillip Morton, this could only be an improvement."

"Phillip? I forget, who is this Phillip?" asked Gigi.

"How could you forget him? The creep who used to call Demi all the time?" Shannon answered.

"He was in one of my classes," said Demi. "A real backwards guy. I felt sorry for him . . ."

"And so you were nice to him," guessed Gigi. "Nice, it is so boring, Demi. You of all people should have known better than that!"

"Gigi, you shock me." Demi held up a sheer black shirt, shook her head, and plunged back into her closet. "Anyway, I've learned my lesson. I thought he'd never stop calling me."

"Well, at least *somebody's* calling you," said Shannon. She sighed.

"Put an ad in CALL ME," suggested Gigi languidly.

"No way," said Shannon. "Demi thinks it's funny, but . . ."

"But there are psychos lurking everywhere?" Demi finished for her. "Don't worry Shannon. If I do meet any sick puppies, I'll give them the name of your kennel."

"Hah, hah," said Shannon.

Yanking a thin black cotton sweater over her head, Demi looked at her watch. "Time to go."

"Demi. You should at least tell us who this guy is and where you're going so if anything happens — "

"I don't believe you, Shannon! What is this? Go on a date and die?"

"She's right," said Gigi unexpectedly. "Shannon, I mean. One cannot be too careful."

Her hand on the doorknob, Demi interrupted impatiently, "Okay, okay. I'll be careful. And I've told you everything I know about him."

With a frown, Shannon said, "But what if he just *said* all that stuff? I mean, what if he isn't really a French major and his name isn't really Lance? What if he's been reading the ads and is just waiting for his chance to kill someone?"

Demi gritted her teeth. "Shannon, the only thing that's gonna kill me on a date like this is boredom, like Gigi said."

Gigi started laughing but Shannon didn't change expression. She just stared at Demi solemnly.

"Hey, Shan? Get over it, okay?" Demi yanked the door and walked out in exasperation.

How did Shannon and I become friends in the first place, Demi wondered as she hurried down the stairs to meet her date. I've got to rethink this friendship. She may be just a little *too* weird for me.

"Mais non. Je t'aime."

"But no, I love you," Lance whispered loudly beside Demi.

"I *know*." Demi hissed back. "I can read the subtitles!"

"Oh, Jacques, Jacques . . ."

"Oh, John, John . . ."

Giving up, Demi leaned back in her seat. How long was this torture going to go on?

You asked for this, she told herself. Besides, as a good reporter, you should be taking notes.

With a loud, long-suffering sigh, Demi closed her eyes.

"Wasn't that great?" asked Lance. A light rain had started to fall, giving the night a faint feel of winter. Demi shivered and shoved her hands up the opposite sleeves of her sweater.

"Great," she said.

"What do you want to do now?"

"Oh. Well, Lance, I don't know. You know, that movie was kind of hard for me to follow. It kind of wore me out, you know?"

Lance stared at Demi. Then he smiled. "You know, I never thought about that. I guess it is kind of hard for someone who doesn't speak French, even with me helping with the translation."

Demi arranged her face into a contrite smile. "I *knew* you'd understand. You know, I've even got a little bit of a headache. But I can see how French could be *fascinating*."

"Yeah, isn't it? We could do it again some time. You know, some of those French comedies are really funny . . . although I personally wonder about the French sense of humor sometimes. You know, they think Jerry Lewis is a genius."

"Really," said Demi, walking back in the direction of her dorm. "Tell me more."

Happily unaware of the yawns Demi was inwardly smothering, Lance launched into a description of the history of French comedy, which lasted all the way back to the dorm. When they reached the front entrance, Demi turned.

"Thanks, Lance. It's been very — educational."

Lance leaned toward her. Quickly, Demi turned her head and his kiss slid off her cheek.

It didn't seem to bother him. He smiled and stepped back. *"Bonsoir, ma petite,"* he said. "I'll call you."

"Bon voyage," said Demi, smiling back.

Lance laughed. "You just wished me a good trip. You're funny!" Still chortling he turned and ambled off down the street.

Demi let the fixed smile slide from her face as she headed upstairs to make notes for her article. "Yeah," she said softly. "Have a good trip. A good *long* trip . . ."

Lance was still thinking about French comedy as he walked home. What sort of French comedy would a girl like Demi like? Or maybe, if not Demi, some other girl. Dating through the CALL ME column hadn't been bad at all. The guys in Colette House — the French house — had all given him grief in various forms of crude and idiomatic French, describing any potential date from the personals column as, at best, *"un chien"* or *"un cheval."* But Demi, with her shining hair and glowing eyes, was a real knockout. And if a girl like Demi would put an ad in CALL ME, who knew what other kinds of girls were out there?

Like that girl in his medieval art history class. . . .

Yes, all in all, it had been a most satisfactory night. His mind wandering dreamily, Lance stepped into the crosswalk of the deserted street in front of Colette House. He never noticed the car waiting there, idling in the shadows. He barely heard the roar of the motor as the car revved to life. He felt no pain as it swept across the blacktop and into his body — only a vague surprise as he flew into the air. *"Mon dieu! Je vais mourir! Zut!"* he thought as lights shattered behind his eyelids and darkness filled his brain.

But in the darkness into which he fell, no one answered.

Chapter 4

"Hello. I saw your ad in CALL ME. My name is Lawrence. I was wondering if you would like to go to a movie and pizza. You can choose the movie and I get to choose at least two of the toppings for the pizza . . . so, call me back, okay?"

Demi turned off the CALL ME answering machine set up in the newspaper office and finished writing down the number that Lawrence had left.

"Hot dates?" a voice said sarcastically from the door.

"You're desperate?" asked Demi, without turning her head. She knew who it was: Marge Smythe, a junior who had just been named editor of the features section.

Marge had hated the idea of Demi's article (probably, thought Demi, because she hadn't come up with it first) and she'd done everything she could to sabotage it. It didn't help, of course, that it was Kevin who had been the deciding vote on whether to pursue it, or that Kevin had endorsed it so enthusiastically.

It didn't help either, that Marge had a thing for Kevin and was crazy jealous of anyone who even spoke to him.

"Very funny." Marge walked into the room and threw herself heavily into the chair behind the features desk.

"Merely an observation," returned Demi, tearing the slip of paper off and folding it into her pack.

"You think you are so cool, don't you," said Marge, glaring at Demi.

Demi shrugged. "What's cool got to do with it?" she asked.

"Kevin's flattered you're doing this article. That's all. Nothing else."

"Listen, Marge, I'm glad Kevin likes it. And *that's* all, okay?"

But Marge wasn't listening. "Kevin's flattered, but *I* think it's more than you can handle."

"What do you mean?" Demi was beginning to lose her temper. "Do you mean you don't think I can write it?"

Marge gave Demi an evil smile. "Oh, you're a competent enough writer. Passable, with the right editing . . . but what if one of those dates you go out on goes wrong? Or what if someone finds out what you're up to? And gets angry? Really, really angry at being made a fool of? You could get into trouble, Demi."

She leaned toward Demi and hissed, *"Really big trouble. . . ."*

"How is anybody going to find out, Marge? Are you going to tell them?" Demi gave Marge glare for glare. "Because if people do find out, everyone's going to know you're the one who told. I'll see to that."

"Will you?" Marge stood up, pushing her long, golden hair back from her face, and narrowing her brown eyes. "Somehow, I don't think so.

"But hey, don't let me cramp your style. Enjoy all those dates with all those losers. And hope something weird *does* happen. Because otherwise, in the hands of a writer like you, this story is going to be dull, dull, dull."

Before Demi could think of a suitable comeback, Marge turned and hurried out of the room.

"Vermin," sputtered Demi. She turned back to her desk, gathering up her books, her mind reeling with rage. "Pond scum," she said. "Loser meat."

"Flotsam? Jetsam. Prismatic piece of garbage?" said a deep voice.

"Oh!" Demi spun around to see Kevin and another guy in the doorway — a guy she had noticed before around campus. Oh, great, Demi, she thought, feeling the blush creeping up her cheeks.

"Who were you talking to, Demi?" Kevin went on smiling.

"Nobody," said Demi, hastily. "I mean, I was just leaving. I came up to, to, you know . . ."

"Oh. Oh, yes." Kevin glanced quickly toward the answering machine and then met Demi's eyes, the laughter deepening in his. Then he said, "Demi, this is Brant, a fellow frat member. Brant, Demi. She's doing an important piece for the paper. Good writer."

Relaxing a little under Kevin's praise, Demi looked at Brant. "Hi," she said.

Call me, she thought.

"Hi," said Brant. He looked around the room. "I like this office. I've heard you have to be crazy to work here, though."

"Not just crazy," said Demi. "Merely crazy isn't enough."

"Certifiable," said Kevin.

"Insane," said Demi.

"Whacked out, around the bend, and going over the cliff," Kevin added.

Brant laughed. "I believe you, I believe you."

The CALL ME line rang. "Hello," said the recorded voice. "You have reached . . ." Hastily, Kevin reached out and turned it down so Brant couldn't hear.

Brant looked at him and lifted an eyebrow. "Secrets, bro?"

"Maybe," said Kevin.

"Well, I have to go," said Demi.

"It's good to see you," said Kevin. "Keep me posted."

"I will," said Demi. "It's good to see you." She turned at the door and gave the two guys her best smile. She let her eyes meet Brant's. "Both of you," she said.

Good grief! How had it gotten so late? Demi looked at her watch, checked it against the clock on the back wall of Vinnie's pizzeria. "I'll meet you there at seven." That's what Lawrence had said, hadn't he? Pizza first and then the movie. It had sounded pleasant and normal enough.

But she'd been sitting here for almost thirty minutes. Had he stood her up? Was this some juvenile guy's idea of a joke? Some fraternity dare? Was he sitting somewhere else in the restaurant now, watching her?

Trying to act casual, she glanced around the room. It was full of a typical Saturday night crowd: a table of frats, several dates, a couple of families, two girls talking intensely in the corner. No one else was there by themselves.

Except her.

What a creep, she thought. Although I suppose it'll make an interesting paragraph in the article.

As if conjured up by the word "creep," Phillip Morton slid into the seat across from her.

"Phillip! What are you doing here?"

"You can call me Lawrence. It's my middle name. Or Phillip."

"*You're* Lawrence? I don't believe this!" Demi didn't know whether to laugh or cry. "You?"

"I couldn't believe it either. I mean, that it was you. But when you called . . ." Phillip smiled smugly.

"This is ridiculous," said Demi, standing up.

Phillip caught her sleeve. "Why? It's a date, like any other date. Give it a shot, Demi."

Reluctantly, Demi allowed herself to be pulled back down. "But why didn't I recognize *your* voice?"

"You told my roommate who it was on the phone. You asked for Lawrence. The only place I'd used that name was answering the CALL

ME ad. So I disguised my voice. Remember, you asked if I had a cold or something?"

"Oh, yeah. Right." Demi looked up as the waiter appeared.

"So, how do you like your pizza?" asked Phillip.

Demi looked across at him, his sandy hair, his freckled nose, his thin mouth, and sighed inwardly. "Anything but anchovies," she said resignedly.

"Decent movie," said Demi as they left the theater. In fact, it hadn't been a bad date, she thought. Not that Phillip ever, in a million years, could be her type. But, still, it had been fine. Just fine.

"Where to now?" asked Phillip. "I have my car."

Demi looked at Phillip in surprise. "It's late," she said.

"It's Saturday night," said Phillip. "It's not that late."

"Late enough," said Demi.

Phillip's face darkened. "Didn't you have a good time?"

"Yes, I did," said Demi honestly. "But now I need to get back to my dorm." She matched her actions to her words, turning to walk in the direction of the campus.

"At least let me drive you," said Phillip.

Yeah, right, thought Demi. Like I'm gonna get in a car with you.

"I'd rather walk," she said aloud. "We can walk and talk, okay?"

"But . . ."

Demi walked on and after a moment, Phillip fell into step beside her. They traveled in silence for several minutes. Then he burst out, "What is it? Do you think you're too good for me? Is that it?"

They'd reached the long, dark sidewalk that snaked across the Commons beneath the massive old oak trees. The globe lights that marked the path glowed like small, pale moons floating in the darkness. If it had been anyone other than Phillip, thought Demi, it would have been romantic.

She kept walking.

"Demi!"

"Phillip, this conversation is pointless. I had a good time. Thank you. But it was a date, not a marriage. Get it?"

"You *do* think you're too good for me!" Phillip grabbed her arm.

Demi pulled free and kept walking.

"Hey," said Phillip. "Hey!"

"I'm going home," said Demi, as levelly as she could.

This time, when Phillip grabbed her arm, it hurt.

"Phillip, let go of me."

"What's wrong with me?" demanded Phillip, his voice rising. "Tell me that."

"Nothing. We're just not . . . right for each other," said Demi, thinking, Puh-leeze. How can you not know what a weirdo you are?

"You don't even like me, do you? Why don't you like me?" Now Phillip's voice sounded almost like a child's. It gave Demi the creeps.

"Let go of me, please, Phillip."

In answer, his grip tightened.

"Phillip."

"Why don't you like me, Demi? Why? *Why?*" He punctuated each question with a jerk on Demi's arm. "Demi?"

Demi lost her temper. "That's it! I've had it, Phillip! You want to know why I don't like you? Because you're a loser! A creep! A nerd! You don't even walk like a normal person, you, you *ooze*. And you don't know when to stop!"

With the strength of anger, Demi pulled her arm away so forcefully that Phillip was knocked off balance. She strode away. After a minute, she heard his footsteps start up after her.

Spinning around she shouted, "Don't you dare! Don't you dare even come near me, you jerk!"

Phillip stopped, his head snapping back as if she'd slapped him.

"Demi," he almost whimpered.

She ignored him. She turned back toward the dorm and kept walking. He didn't follow her this time. But when she looked over her shoulder as she left the walkway, she thought she could still see him standing amidst the trees, watching her, a lonely, ghostly figure in the shadows.

Chapter 5

The phone was ringing.

Demi groaned. Who would call her at such an ungodly hour on a Sunday morning?

"Go away," she muttered. "Die."

The phone kept ringing.

Why didn't someone answer it? Where was her roommate?

Ring. Rinnnnnng.

"Agggh," cried Demi, sitting up and hurling her pillow in the direction of the sound.

Of course she missed.

Giving up, Demi got out of her narrow dorm bed and stumbled over to the phone.

"Hello?" she croaked.

"Demi? Is that you?"

"Barely," she said crossly. "Who's this?"

"Kevin," said the voice, sounding surprised.

"Kev — oh, Kevin. Hi." She tried to make her voice sound a little friendlier.

"Did I wake you up?"

"Yes, but, ah, no problem. I mean, *is* there some kind of problem? It's kinda early."

"I just wanted to know how everything went last night."

"Last night? Oh, the features article project. God, Kevin, don't you ever stop working?"

"Working is my life," answered Kevin, only half joking.

"Well, it was a bummer, but it'll make a good bit for the article," said Demi.

Kevin's voice sharpened. "Bummer? What happened?"

"Nothing. No big deal. A footnote for the article, at best." Resolutely, Demi pushed the image of Phillip's lonely figure standing in the shadows out of her mind.

"You sure?"

"Kevin . . ."

"Sorry, Demi. I know you can handle it. But how many more of these bogus dates are you going to have?"

Demi laughed. "Not many. How many do you think I need for the piece?"

"Good question." Kevin was silent a moment. "Listen, sorry I woke you up. Gimme a call when you feel like it and we'll talk."

"Great," said Demi. "See ya."

She hung up the phone and stumbled sleepily

back to bed. She'd barely closed her eyes when the phone rang again.

"What *is* this? The Torture Demi on Sunday Morning Show?" she said aloud. She got back out of bed, stomped across the room, and snatched up the phone.

"Hello!" she growled.

"Demi? Demi Blake?"

She didn't recognize the voice. It was older and official sounding.

Demi cleared her throat and said, cautiously, "Who's calling please?"

"This is Officer Elizabeth DeVito with the Salem police department. We'd like to talk to you."

"What? Is this some kind of joke?"

"Is this Ms. Blake?"

"Yes," Demi admitted. "But how do I know you're really a cop?"

"Ms. Blake, we are downstairs at your dormitory. We have your resident adviser with us. Could you come down, or should we come up?"

"What's going on? What's wrong?"

"We can discuss that when we see you, Ms. Blake."

"Okay." Demi was wide awake now, her mind racing. "Okay, I'll be right down."

Ten minutes later, feeling scattered and

somehow panicky, Demi was sitting in a chair in the Quad lounge where the resident advisor had left her with Officer DeVito and her partner, Officer Chang.

"So what's this all about?" asked Demi.

It was Officer Chang who answered, leaning forward to peer at Demi intently. "Do you know a Phillip Lawrence Morton?"

"Phillip? Sure," said Demi. "Why?"

"When did you last see Phillip, Ms. Blake?" That was Officer DeVito.

Demi looked from one to the other. "Last night. We had a date."

Officer DeVito continued, making notes in her notebook. "Can you tell us what you did on that date?"

"Pizza, a movie, then he walked me home."

"And about what time was that?"

"I don't know. Eleven, eleven-thirty."

"Did anything unusual happen on this date you had with Phillip?"

"No! I mean, it was just an ordinary date, I guess. I mean, we'd never gone out before or anything." Something made Demi keep quiet about the date's disastrous ending. "Officer DeVito, could you please tell me what this is all about?"

Officer Chang answered, watching Demi intently. Demi could feel Officer DeVito's gaze on her, too.

"Last night, sometime around midnight, Phillip went to his car, in a closed garage. He was found early this morning in the car, unconscious, with the motor running."

"What?" Demi gasped. "Phillip!"

"We are trying to determine if this was a suicide attempt or if there is some other explanation. Phillip sustained a blow to the head which may have been caused when he became unconscious and fell against the dashboard. Or it may have been delivered before."

"Before? What are you saying? That someone hit Phillip and put him in the car and left him?"

"Is that what you think happened, Demi?" asked Officer Chang.

"No. That's crazy! That's, that's like *murder*."

Silence.

Finally, Officer DeVito said, "We have not ruled out the possibility of foul play. Nor of suicide. Ms. Blake, did Phillip say anything that might shed some light on why he might try to commit suicide?"

Demi suddenly saw the lonely, ghostly figure on the path, heard her own angry words. Was it possible she had caused Phillip to do such a terrible thing?

No. No, it couldn't be. She looked at each officer in turn before answering firmly, "Nothing happened. It was just an ordinary date."

"I don't believe it!"

"Believe it. It's true." Demi cradled the cup of coffee in her hands. Around them, the caf was relatively quiet. The few other students who were up so early on a Sunday morning were reading newspapers, talking quietly, or staring sleepily off into space.

"Wow." Shannon's eyes sparkled with a sort of hungry excitement. "Do you think, you know, you tipped him over the edge?"

Shannon's words were so close to Demi's own guilty thoughts that she answered more vehemently than she meant to. "No! Of course not!"

Shannon didn't seem to notice. She thought for a moment, then said, almost as if she were disappointed, "No, probably not."

"It was some kind of an accident," Demi said.

"Yeah." Shannon's eyes suddenly sparkled with suppressed excitement. "Or — what if it really *was* something else. You know."

"Attempted murder? I don't think so." Demi shook her head, trying to clear it. Which was worse? Suicide, or murder? There was no answer. At least Phillip wasn't dead. He was unconscious, but they said he would be all right. They'd know more when he came to. They'd find out it was an accident.

"Are you freaked?" Shannon asked, her eyes sparkling even more.

"What do you think?" asked Demi rudely.

"You want to know what I think?" Shannon looked around them and even though no one was near, she lowered her voice dramatically. "I think it's a sign."

"A sign? A sign of what?"

"That you shouldn't be doing this date thing. I mean, at least, not for the newspaper."

"Shannon, you are acting world-class weird, you know that? Why shouldn't I do this? Are you still wigged I took your dare?"

"Demi! No. It's just that it's so cold. It's like, using people, you know?"

"Why? Who's to say I might not meet someone I really like?"

"And what about Jack? He's crazy jealous of you," Shannon pointed out.

"Since when do you care what Jack thinks?"

Shannon shrugged. "He's a nice guy, that's all. And cute."

Demi pushed her coffee cup away impatiently. "Nice. Cute. Puppies and kittens are nice and cute. I want something more."

"Don't be greedy, Demi."

Standing up, Demi looked down at Shannon. "Greedy? What do you mean by that?"

The excited look left Shannon's eyes. They suddenly turned dark and troubled. "You know, you're used to getting everything you want. But sometimes, getting what you want — it can cost you."

"Oooh, heavy," mocked Demi. "Listen, I can take care of myself. I'm not going to give up on this article. Or on anything else I want. *And no one can make me.*"

But a few hours later, sitting at the features desk in the *Chronicle* office, Demi wasn't so sure. The day had gone slack and gray outside, with a sort of sullen mugginess that was getting on her nerves.

It can cost you. Demi kept thinking about Shannon's words. It wasn't like Shannon to be so serious. But then, how well did she know Shannon, really? Just that she was fun and funny and easy to get along with. Who was to say that Shannon didn't have a dark side — as dark as whatever had driven Phillip to do what he had done?

No. No, it was an accident. "An accident," she said aloud, resolutely. She reached for the folder of notes and releases for the regular features in the newspaper and opened it to begin sorting them. Marge had given Demi that assignment when Demi had joined the paper. It was tedious, and time-consuming, but Demi supposed that it *was* good training, just as Marge had said in her nasty voice before giving Demi the job.

Police Notes, Demi typed into the computer. She sighed and went through the blotter, pulling out the things that pertained to the Salem U. campus.

A petty theft from a dorm. A stolen bicycle. A police course in self-defense. A hit and run.

Demi stopped. Her eyes widened.

Lance?

In disbelief, she read the police report. The night of their date, as Lance was going home, someone had hit him. And kept driving. Witnesses had heard the accident, but no one had seen anything.

The police were still investigating.

Lance was in critical condition at the Twin Falls hospital.

"No," Demi breathed.

But it was true. On the night of their date, Lance, like Phillip, had very nearly lost his life.

Chapter 6

"Well, well, well, if it isn't our little Connie Chung, star reporter." Marge, of course.

Instinctively, Demi covered the sheet of paper she'd been reading with her hand.

"Demi," said Kevin, coming in on Marge's heels. His face broke into a grin. "I was hoping you'd be here."

Forcing herself to smile in answer, Demi said lightly, "You can't keep me away from the newspaper!"

"A woman after my own heart," said Kevin, his eyes warm with approval.

"We can't stay long," said Marge. "We're on our way *out*." She put her hand possessively on Kevin's arm.

Seemingly unaware of Marge's animosity, Kevin said, "Marge, why don't you go on? I'll meet you downstairs."

"I don't mind waiting here," said Marge.

"Yeah, but I need to talk to Demi and the car is parked in ticketland out front. You'd be doing me a big favor if you'd keep an eye on it, maybe move it if the cops come along."

Torn between wanting to stay and keep Demi from being alone with Kevin, and doing what he asked, Marge at last said, "Okay. See you *soon.*"

"Bye, Marge," said Demi.

Marge walked out without answering.

Turning immediately back to Demi, Kevin said, "What's wrong?"

"What makes you think something is wrong?" countered Demi.

"Demi, I can see it in your face."

"You can?" Demi was surprised. She prided herself on being able to conceal her feelings. I must be more upset than I want to admit, she thought.

"Demi?"

"Look," she said, thrusting the police report toward Kevin. He read it slowly.

"I don't get it," said Kevin.

"Lance is the first guy I went out with from CALL ME. And it happened the night of our date. Right after it, it sounds like."

"It's a bad coincidence, but . . ."

"And it's happened again!" Demi burst out. "The guy I went out with last night? Phillip?

43

They found him in his car this morning, with the motor running." Quickly she told Kevin about the visit from the police.

When she was finished, Kevin shook his head. "It's bad. But — is he dead?"

"N-no. He's unconscious. In the hospital."

"And they don't know what happened?"

"No. I told you. Suicide. An accident, maybe even . . ."

"Murder?" said Kevin quickly. "It's not possible! I mean, do they have any clues?"

"I don't know. I don't think so. They kept asking me questions. It was awful."

Kevin reached out and put his hands on Demi's shoulders. "Demi. Get a grip. It's not your fault."

"But both guys! How could something terrible happen to both people I went out with?"

"Do the cops know? About your going out with Lance *and* Phillip before these things happened?"

"No! Just Phillip. I didn't tell them about Lance. I mean, it sounds so crazy. So sick and crazy." Demi looked down at the paper she was holding and realized her hand was shaking. Carefully, she put the paper down. Kevin's hands on her shoulders felt good. For a moment she had an impulse to lean against him and close her eyes and feel safe.

But it would have been a bogus safety.

Instead she stepped back and looked up into Kevin's eyes. "Do you think it's connected, Kevin?"

"No, of course I don't," said Kevin soothingly. "I'm sure it's just a random thing. A wild coincidence."

Was Kevin being honest? His expression was open, reassuring. Demi found herself wanting to believe him.

Then Kevin frowned. "But still, maybe you should just scratch this CALL ME piece. For the time being, anyway."

"No! No, I want to do it."

"Are you sure? Think about it, Demi. Maybe it would be for the best . . ."

"Listen, it's only a few more dates. Then I'll have enough material for a decent feature." Demi was beginning to regain her sense of balance. "In fact, it's going to be a *great* story."

"You *like* doing this?" Kevin looked incredulous. "From the little you've told me about it, it sounds pretty grueling. Or is there something you're not telling me?" he added more lightly, trying to make her smile.

"Maybe," she said, trying to match her tone to his. "Hey, it's a dirty job, Kev. But someone's got to do it."

Taking a deep breath, Kevin said, "You're

tough, Demi. Listen, if you need my help, you want to talk more about this, whatever, give me a call. Promise me that."

Impulsively, Demi reached up and kissed Kevin on the cheek. "Thanks, Kevin. I will." She watched in surprise as a faint blush crept up Kevin's cheeks.

"Demi," he began. But before he could go on, the raucous sound of a horn blaring broke into the moment.

"I think I hear someone calling you," said Demi.

Kevin grinned ruefully. "I think you're right. But remember, you can call me." He grabbed a couple of folders from his desk and hurried out of the room.

"CALL ME," said the voice. Demi cocked her head, listening to the message. She'd put the police report back in the file, written up the feature notes, and put the hard copy on Marge's desk. Marge would mark it up viciously before returning it to Demi for a largely unnecessary rewrite, but at least that was done.

"I'm answering the CALL ME ad for a night I'll never forget. I think I can give you a night *you'll* never forget. My name is Andrew and here's my number."

Demi wrote it down, shaking her head. Whoever this Andrew was, he didn't have an ego problem.

Heading back toward the dorm, she kept yawning. The day had been long and hard. She was glad she didn't have any plans for that night. She was going to grab some dinner, then take it easy. Go to bed early, even.

She'd earned it.

"Call me."

"Hello?" said Demi.

Why didn't you call me?" asked the voice at the other end of the phone.

"Who is this?" asked Demi. "How did you get my number?"

"You had your chance," the voice intoned.

"Who *are* you?"

"Your dream date, Demi. Don't you know who I am?"

"I don't have to listen to this!" Demi slammed the phone down, hard.

But the voice went on.

"You had your chance. Now you have to pay."

The room spun. Everything in it seemed to be moving. To have a life of its own.

Then Demi realized she was holding something in her hand. The *Chronicle*.

With her picture on the front page. Why? What was happening?

Then she saw the headline: KILLER DATE.

"No," gasped Demi.

The voice began to laugh. It came from nowhere.

It came from everywhere.

"Who are you?" cried Demi.

The laughter grew and grew

She had to get out of there. She had to find the door before she drowned in the monstrous laughter.

The door . . .

Demi began to run toward the door. Slowly. So slowly. When she tripped, she seemed to fall forever.

She landed softly.

She'd fallen on something. Something warm and alive.

But barely. Just barely.

Lance.

No.

Phillip?

But how could it be?

"Who are you?" she gasped.

The thing on the floor rolled over. Opened its mouth. Blood gushed out as it spoke.

"Call me," it whispered.

Chapter 7

"Noooo!" screamed Demi.

And woke up.

The morning sun was streaming through the window.

Her roommate had already left for an early class.

Demi groaned and put her hands to her aching head. She didn't even remember falling asleep.

At least I slept through the night, she thought wryly. She got up slowly and went down to the Dungeon, the series of underground tunnels that ran beneath the Quad. The coffee she got from the machine was vile, but hot. She bought two cups and made her way slowly back up to her room, the nightmare still scalded in her mind.

"What have I done to deserve this?" she said aloud softly.

No one answered. Crossing to the window, she leaned on the sill and looked out. Below, students hurried to class. Tender green leaves no bigger than a thumb were budding on the trees. The skyline of Salem U. was etched against a soft blue sky, the clock tower standing benignly above it all like a finger pointed to heaven.

Although she would never be so disgustingly sentimental as to admit it, Demi loved Salem. It was her kingdom, her world, at least for the next few years. She wanted to leave her mark on it, to have people remember her, wanted to come back some day and have people point and say, "That's Demi Blake. She's famous, you know. Everyone knew she was going to be, even when she was a student here."

But famous for what? For having every guy she went out with meet a bad end?

Shake it off, Demi, she told herself. She took a slurp of bitter coffee and let her gaze wander the skyline: Abbey House, the trees of the Commons, the distant outcrop of restaurants and stores along Pennsylvania Avenue.

And there, barely discernible, the brooding gray silhouette of Nightingale Hall.

Nightmare Hall.

You wouldn't know what it was unless you knew to look for it. You would think it was just another jigsaw bit of building stuck in the Salem skyline.

But it wasn't.

Nightmare Hall.

Had the poor girl who died been haunted like this? Had she had bad dreams?

Nightmares?

Involuntarily, Demi turned her head away and shuddered. Stop it, Demi, she told herself. It's not the same thing. You just had a bad dream. And a little bad luck.

And bad luck at one remove really. Because it wasn't she, Demi, who was in the hospital. It was Lance and Phillip.

Two separate people who had had two separate, unrelated things happen to them. Things that had nothing to do with her.

Demi finished her coffee. Salem waited below. Safe. Sane. Normal.

Just like me, thought Demi. It's time to get ready to cruise the ivied halls of normalcy. Time for a day just like any other.

In fact, maybe the nightmare had been a good thing. Maybe it would help her shake off all her weird fears, help her see that strange coincidences did happen.

Yes. Already she was feeling better.

And that was that.

Demi finished her coffee and raised the

empty cup in a toast to Salem campus and the new day.

"Hey babe."

Demi, who had been waiting impatiently in front of the Quad for fifteen minutes, made an elaborate show of looking over her shoulder.

The tanned, dark-haired boy in the expensive little red car with the top folded down looked momentarily annoyed. Then a practiced smile replaced the look, revealing perfect white teeth.

Too perfect, thought Demi. My what big teeth you have, Grandma.

"You. Demi?" said the boy.

"That's my name," said Demi. "I usually answer to it."

Then she thought, tone it down, girl, or this date will never start.

She gave Andrew Decker Winston III a smile as practiced as the one he'd given her. "You must be Andrew." *Babe*.

Andrew leaned across the seat of the car and pushed the door open. "I did this little dating thing as a joke. My frat bros and I thought it would be a hoot."

Demi slid into the seat, watching Andrew stare at the hem of her short skirt as it attempted to ride up her thigh. But she caught it in time and folded herself neatly into place in the low seat. As she did, Andrew leaned back across her, staying in the position just a fraction longer than he needed to in order to close the door.

"Thanks," said Demi with false sweetness. "You were saying I'm part of a joke?"

Unfazed, Andrew answered, "Yeah, but wait'll the guys hear about you. You're no joke."

He jammed the car into gear and they ripped away from the curb, causing people to turn and stare.

"We're going to the movies," announced Andrew as if he were bestowing a gift on Demi. "Clint Eastwood. I love him, y'know? My father, he likes John Wayne. I guess you could say it runs in the family." Andrew threw his head back and laughed heartily at his own joke, oblivious to the fact that Demi didn't join in.

"A movie," said Demi neutrally. What an original choice. Take note for the piece: there are other date ideas out there, guys!

"Of course, my father likes Clint, too," Andrew confided.

"Your father. That would be Andrew Decker Winston II?"

"Yeah!" Andrew threw Demi a surprised look. "You know him?"

"Just an educated guess," said Demi.

"Oh," said Andrew. "One of those intellectual babes, huh?"

"I'm not — " Demi began, but she never got to finish telling Andrew not to call her — or any woman — a babe. He rolled on.

"Hey, that's okay with me. I like smart girls. My father says . . ."

Resigned, Demi leaned her head back and looked up at the sky. At least it was a great car and she liked being able to lean back and let the wind brush her face. She didn't really mind Clint Eastwood, either.

And it wasn't like she had to make conversation. Andrew was having a great conversation with himself.

She realized as she walked into the movie theater with Andrew that part of the joke was to have been Andrew's frat brothers sharing in the whole date, at least vicariously. Although she pretended not to notice, Demi caught the exchange of looks between Andrew and a small group of guys standing near the refreshment stand, and the fake double takes and elaborate nudges the guys performed as she and Andrew walked by.

"Friends of yours?" she couldn't resist asking when they'd passed.

Andrew at least had the grace to look

abashed. "Oh, um, yeah, I see them around campus sometimes. You want any popcorn or anything?"

You want to go talk to your frat bros? she thought. "Sure," said Demi. "I like whatever you like."

Andrew made his escape and Demi settled in for the movie. What was Andrew talking to his frat brothers about? She could just imagine.

Oh, well. At least Andrew would make good copy in her article.

Moments before the movie started, Andrew sat down by her, holding a huge bucket of heavily buttered popcorn and two sodas. He handed a soda and the popcorn to her and then began to eat loudly from the bucket.

"You can hold the popcorn," Demi said at last.

"No, thanks," said Andrew, continuing to eat. He crunched and munched all the way through the movie.

"Great movie, huh," he said as they left the theater.

"Great," said Demi. She caught herself looking surreptitiously around the theater, scoping for Andrew's buddies. But they must not have liked their joke backfiring on them. They were nowhere to be seen.

"I know a great steak house," said Andrew

when they'd gotten back to his car.

"It's kinda late," said Demi. She might as well have been talking to the door. Andrew pulled out of the parking lot with a scream of tires and sped away from the campus. They roared out of town, then turned off onto a winding, two-lane road. The stripes in the middle of the road flashed by faster and faster as they got farther and farther from town.

"Andrew?" said Demi.

He didn't seem to hear.

"Andrew!"

The tires of the car screamed as they rounded a corner.

"I love this car, babe!" shouted Andrew

"I'm not a babe!" cried Demi. "Not your babe. Not anybody's babe!"

They were climbing a hill now. Andrew didn't answer. With a look of concentration on his face, he floored the accelerator. The car gave a little jerk, then leaped forward. They hit the top of the hill. Headlights blinded Demi.

"Look outtttt!" she screamed.

Then they were flying through the air.

Chapter 8

The car flew higher. Jagged treetops clawed the headlights.

Then they came down with a sickening thud as another car swerved by them and careened into the night, the blast of an angry horn trailing away from it.

"Wasn't that great!" shouted Andrew. "This baby can really hold the road, can't she?"

"Are you crazy?" screamed Demi. "We were almost killed!"

"No way." Andrew turned down another narrower, darker road without slowing down. "That curve just seems like that. I know this road like the back of my hand. I told you, this is my favorite steak joint. Nick's. Nick's in the Sticks. . . . "

He threw back his head and laughed hugely.

"Watch the road!" shouted Demi desperately.

Surprisingly, he slowed down. At least he listens to me a little, thought Demi. Until she realized that they'd reached the restaurant.

Andrew sniffed the air and cut the engine. "Meat!" he said. "C'mon, babe."

This has been the longest night of my life, thought Demi, as Andrew drove them back to town after dinner. She'd watched him consume what seemed like pounds and pounds of virtually raw beef and a huge plate of fries. When she hadn't eaten the huge sirloin he'd ordered for her, he'd eaten that, too.

Sickening.

Maybe I'm going to be sick now, Demi's thoughts went on. That would get Dandy Andy's attention.

No. She stifled a groan and closed her eyes while Andrew skidded the car around yet another curve.

I can take this, she thought. I've had worse dates.

Too bad she couldn't remember any. . . .

"We're heeeere," said Andrew.

Demi opened her eyes. They were in an almost empty, bottle-strewn parking lot outside a long, low cinder-block building with narrow, dark windows. Boarded-up buildings and empty lots filled with shuffling pieces of newspaper surrounded them.

"Here, where, exactly?" Demi asked carefully.

"The best little pool hall in town. I like to shoot pool. You'll like it too."

"What I'd like," said Demi through gritted teeth, "is to go home."

"Home." Andrew laughed his huge, annoying laugh. "Good one, babe. The night's early. C'mon."

"*No*, Andrew. Watch my lips. Take me home."

In the act of leaning across Demi to open the door, Andrew stopped.

"Are you serious?"

His face loomed in front of her like a demented moon. Demi closed her eyes again. "I've never been more serious in my life."

Closing her eyes was a big mistake. The next thing Demi knew, Andrew was pressed against her, his mouth mashed against hers.

"Wh-mmm-uh!" Demi tried to pull free. Andrew threw one bear-like arm across her and kept on kissing her.

"Mmm-hhhhuh-ah! Andrew, stop!"

Andrew pulled back slightly, took a deep breath, then dove toward Demi again.

"You *are* crazy!" With all her strength, Demi

pushed Andrew away. He lurched sideways. She heard him hit the gearshift and begin to howl in pain.

She waited until she'd gotten out of the car before turning to ask, "Are you okay?"

Andrew was doubled over in his seat. Now it was his turn, she noted with satisfaction, to talk through gritted teeth.

He straightened up slightly. The look on his face in the dim light from above the door of the pool hall made Demi step back.

"You . . ." he grated. "I take you out, a loser babe so desperate she has to get dates in a personals column. And this is the thanks I get."

"W-hat?" Demi felt her jaw drop.

"Wait'll the brothers hear about this. You'll never have a date in this town again."

"I don't need your help getting a date!"

Andrew straightened up a little more. "No? Well then maybe you don't need my help getting home."

Before Demi could react, Andrew switched on the ignition of his car, threw it into gear with a shriek of metal, and lurched out of the parking lot.

"I don't believe this," said Demi.

She looked around the parking lot.

"Believe it," she answered herself and began

to walk resolutely toward the pool hall to call a cab to take her home.

"Demi! I don't believe it!"

Demi put her hands over her ears. "Don't shout. You're giving me a headache."

Gigi, in the act of reaching into the microwave in the dorm lounge where the three girls had drifted by unspoken agreement, said, "Do not go out on any more of these dates, Demi. After a night like tonight? No, no, no, I do not think they are good for you." She opened the steaming bag and dumped the popcorn into a bowl.

Shaking her head, Shannon said, "Not good for her is putting it mildly. Do you know, do you have any *idea* what kind of damage someone like Andrew can do to you, Demi? I mean, talk about bad-luck dates! Too bad it's not Andrew who — "

"Shannon!" Demi glared at Shannon in exasperation. Couldn't Shannon keep anything a secret? So far, Demi had been able to keep the story of her dates with Phillip and Lance vague. And no one had connected what had happened to them to her.

But of course, she'd confided in Shannon. Shannon was her friend. That's what friends were for.

Or was it? If Shannon couldn't keep something like this a secret, how could she be trusted with anything? Although, Demi thought, she was never so indiscreet before. It's almost like she wants to tell everyone I'm some kind of bad-luck date . . .

Realizing that Gigi was looking from one to the other of them with bright-eyed curiosity, Demi reached for the bowl of popcorn. "Too bad it's not Andrew who what, Shannon?"

Shannon had the grace to blush. "To, uh, ask me out. He's only in the best fraternity on campus!"

Gigi wrinkled her nose. "Me, I do not like fraternities. It makes boys more than ever act like children."

Shannon giggled and Demi couldn't help but smile. Gigi's perspective on guys was somehow reassuring. Even Andrew's behavior didn't seem so outrageous when she thought of it as childish.

"Boys," said Demi, shaking her head. "You can't live with 'em and you can't live without 'em."

But Gigi had the last word. With a characteristic shrug, she said, "But no. It is not that way at all. They cannot live without us, poor things."

The three girls collapsed with laughter.

Demi was still laughing when she strolled back into her room. Her roommate, she saw, was still out on *her* date with her steady boyfriend.

"Better luck on yours," muttered Demi. She pulled out her notebook so she could make notes on the evening for her article while events were still fresh in her mind. Not, she thought wryly, that she was likely to forget an evening like this one. She wondered if Andrew would read the article and recognize himself in it. She smiled at the thought. His portrait would be particularly unflattering. No, not unflattering — accurate.

Put that in your ego and cook with it, Andrew, she told him silently.

In a way, it was inspirational.

Revenge could be sweet.

She was so intent on her work that she answered for the phone almost absentmindedly when it rang, never thinking how odd it would be that someone would be calling so late on a Saturday night.

"Hello?" she said.

"Hello, Demi," the strange breathy voice at the other end of the line said. "Working late tonight?"

"Who is this?"

"And still wearing that yellow sweater. I like that sweater on you, Demi."

Demi looked down at the yellow v-neck sweater she'd worn on her date with Andrew.

"Did he like that sweater on you, Demi?"

"How did you . . . who are you?"

The voice changed suddenly.

"Demi, Demi, telling lies.

"Kissed the boys and made them . . ."

It rose to a shriek:

"DIEEEEEEEEE!"

Chapter 9

The corridors stretched on forever: gleaming, white, sterile.

Dead.

No. Not dead.

Not dead yet, Demi told herself.

She stepped back to let an orderly wheeling an empty trolley pass. A trolley stained with blood.

Quickly she closed her eyes. Took a deep breath.

What am I doing here? she thought.

It's a nightmare.

But it wasn't. It was real.

It was the night before that had been the nightmare. She'd slammed down the phone with shaking hands, the demonic shriek ringing in her ears.

Dieeeeeee.

Die.

She'd torn off the yellow sweater with shaking hands, then realized that the dorm window curtains were open. Turning off the lights so no one outside could see into her room, she'd leaped across to close the curtains.

And to peer down three stories into the well of darkness below. Only it hadn't been a well of darkness. It had been a perfectly normal, well-lit street wending its way among stately oaks and maples and venerable old buildings. A postcard of a typical college evening. As she had stood there a couple had walked by, holding hands, laughing. They'd stopped to kiss just at the edge of the circle of gold cast by the streetlight. Then they'd continued on, laughing, happy.

Normal.

No one else had been down there. No one was lurking below, watching her window.

And beyond the trees, above the streetlight, the familiar Salem skyline, distant windows and distant lights, like the beacons on some lee shore.

Unbidden, Demi had suddenly remembered the opening scene in the classic movie *Jaws*, where the girl had swum out into the dark water. The first time the shark had hit her, the girl hadn't even known what it was. She'd treaded water there, the peaceful lights of the safe shore not so far away.

Only they had been far away — too far for that girl to ever reach again.

Abruptly Demi had turned away from the window.

What is going on, she'd wondered. Am I going crazy?

Or is someone crazy going after me?

Her thoughts in a tangle, she'd gotten ready for bed. Left the light in the bathroom on so she wouldn't be in the dark. Laid down and pulled the covers up over her head like a little kid.

As Demi stood in the long, empty corridor, she went over it all one more time. Had what happened to Lance and Phillip been more than bad luck, nasty coincidence? Had she, somehow, been responsible for what had happened to them?

Or was someone just trying to make her paranoid? Trying to get revenge for some real or imagined slight?

But who?

Immediately Demi thought of Jack.

Jack, who hadn't called her since that last disastrous meeting at Mort par Chocolat. Jack, who'd been so possessive, so jealous.

So angry.

Jack knew she was doing the dating thing.

Had Jack somehow found out, or figured out what had happened? Then called her to pay her back for breaking up with him?

But Jack would never do something like that. Would he?

She'd frowned, trying to recall the exact sound of the muffled, obviously disguised voice on the phone. It *could* have been Jack. But then, it could have been anyone. Hard to tell, even, whether it was male or female.

Female.

Marge.

Marge who matched Jack for jealous behavior. Who truly hated Demi. Who imagined that she was after the one guy Marge wanted.

Easy enough for Marge to listen to the answering machine in the *Chronicle* office and find out who Demi had gone out with. To put two and two together.

To make a threatening phone call.

But how had Marge known what she was wearing?

Whoever had called had known that. Which meant that whoever had called had to have seen her earlier in the evening.

Who had she seen? Gigi, Shannon. Half a dozen other girls in her dorm. Andrew. His frat brothers.

Andrew.

Andrew was definitely a creep. An ego monster to the max. Andrew, she was sure, was capable of making a threatening phone call.

But how had Andrew known about Lance and Phillip? Could his words — if it had been him — just been random? Lucky, cruel guesses.

Demi felt a chill creep over her.

Unless it wasn't Andrew. Unless whoever it was had been following her. Had been watching her.

Stalking her.

But if that were true, maybe what had happened to Lance and to Phillip wasn't accidental.

Maybe someone was after her. Maybe the caller was telling the truth.

No one was dead yet.

But maybe *she* was the one who would be the first to die.

"Excuse me? Excuse me, miss?" Demi opened her eyes to meet the concerned eyes of a nurse.

"Are you all right?" the nurse asked.

No, Demi wanted to scream. No, I'm not all right. Something crazy, something terrible and unbelievable is happening to me.

But then, in a hospital, the nurse probably heard that all the time.

Demi forced herself to smile at him. He looked so kind and reassuring. It almost made her feel better.

Almost.

"I'm fine," she said. "Really. I'm just a little — uncomfortable in hospitals."

"If you need to sit down," said the nurse, "there's a lounge at the end of the hall. Would you like for me to walk you down to it?"

"N-no. No thanks. I'll go and get some water though."

The nurse nodded approvingly. "Good idea," he said. "If you need anything, the nurses' station is right around the corner."

"Thanks." Demi went down to the lounge and drank a glass of water. It did make her feel better.

Time to do what she'd come to do.

Time to visit Lance and Phillip.

The door to Lance's room was half-open. He'd been moved out of intensive care and into a semiprivate room. The bed closest to the door was empty. Lance was lying in the bed by the window, encased in bandages.

Walking quietly in, Demi shut the door behind her. "Lance?" she said softly.

The figure on the bed didn't move.

"Lance?"

She crept closer, afraid to waken him, afraid not to. So many questions.

So little time.

Lance stirred. Groaned slightly.

"Lance?" she said a third time, more firmly.

He turned his head. It was a shocking sight. The bandage around his head hid most of his face, covering one eye. His nose had obviously been broken. His lips were swollen and the eye she could see was purple-black.

"Oh, Lance," gasped Demi involuntarily.

Incredibly, his face brightened. "Hello," he croaked.

"You remember me?"

"*Bonjour, belle fille . . .*" Lance stopped and frowned. "Y-yes," he said uncertainly.

"I'm Demi. We had a date. The night — the night this happened."

Lance kept frowning. Then he said, "Demi."

"Demi. Yes. Remember? We went to the movies. A French movie. You translated for me."

"Demi," said Lance with more assurance. "Demi."

"What happened, Lance? That night after you left me at the Quad?"

"Demi," repeated Lance, slowly.

"Yes," Demi said. "We're talking about the

accident. Remember? When the car hit you. *After* our date."

Lance frowned again. "Accident." He took a deep, obviously painful breath. "I don't remember."

"Try, Lance. It's important. Very, very important."

Demi leaned over the bed tensely, staring down at Lance, willing him to remember something, anything. But it was no use.

Slowly, awkwardly, Lance shook his head. "No. I'm sorry. I can't. I can't . . ."

The door opened. "Time for our lunch," a voice sang out cheerily. "Oh, good. You've got company. Is this your girlfriend, dearie?"

"We're just friends," said Demi. "I've got to go. Take care, Lance, okay? Good-bye."

Lance looked up at her sadly. *"Au revoir,"* he said.

A police officer in a blue uniform was sitting in a chair outside Phillip's room.

Startled and shaken, Demi stopped. Then, realizing she looked odd standing in the middle of the hall staring, she walked on, pretending she was headed for some other destination. As she walked past the officer, she stole a glance at Phillip's door. It was closed tightly. A sign on the door said, "No entry without authorization."

Demi walked further down the hall and saw the nurse she'd spoken to earlier.

She smiled and he smiled back. "You're looking better," he said.

"The water helped. And so did you," said Demi. "Thank you again."

"You're welcome."

Demi glanced over her shoulder and looked back at the nurse. She made her eyes wide. "Wow, a policeman. Is there a criminal in there?"

The nurse smiled and shook his head. "Hardly. Just a kid. A boy from Salem. At first they thought he was a suicide, but now they think someone tried to kill him."

"Kill him?" gasped Demi, only half-acting. "Really?"

"Yeah. Hit him on the head, left him in the car with the motor running. Good thing someone came along when they did. Five more minutes and he would have been dead."

"Has he told them who did it?"

The nurse shook his head again. "No. He's only been conscious a couple of times. He is very fragile. It's a terrible thing."

"What are they going to do?"

The nurse patted Demi on the shoulder.

"Don't worry. It'll be okay. And they'll do what we all have to do sometimes, the hardest thing of all."

"What's that?" asked Demi.

The nurse smiled ruefully, the wrinkles around his eyes deepening. "Wait," he said. "Wait and see."

Chapter 10

The day had turned cold and gray. But the steamy-windowed hubbub of the Caf in the late Sunday rush had been too much for Demi to take. She ordered a hot chocolate and took it out to the terrace of the Student Center. Sitting on the wall overlooking the Commons, she wondered dully where the spring had suddenly gone.

Only a few days ago, the sun had been bright and warm, the leaves brave flags of green unfurling from every tree. Now they seemed dull, their colors diluting and dissolving in the wind and rain. The damp cold, winter, making a final, vain attempt to stay alive, seemed to be rising like a miasma from the sodden ground.

Foul play. Attempted murder.

Kiss the boys and make them die . . .

She hunched down in her jacket, cupping the hot chocolate between her hands. She took a sweet, scalding sip, but it didn't warm her.

I didn't do anything, she thought. What did I do?

What have I done to deserve this? Who would hate me so much?

As if in answer to her question, a nasal, sarcastic voice spoke at her shoulder.

"Extra, extra, read all about it."

The latest copy of the local Twin Falls newspaper landed with a thud on the terrace beside Demi.

She jumped in spite of herself.

"Check out the headline, Lois Lane." Marge put a booted foot up on the wall next to Demi.

Demi looked down.

MISSING? read the headline.

Below was a photograph of Andrew.

"What?" cried Demi. She set the chocolate down so hard it sloshed over, burning her hands. But she didn't even notice. She grabbed the newspaper and held it up to read it.

Marge watched Demi, a funny look on her face. After a moment she drawled, "I know you're a news junkie, Demi, but aren't you overreacting? Or is this a case you're going to solve? Your chance for a big scoop?"

Ignoring her, Demi read the article disbelievingly.

But it was true. Andrew, who had gone out

on a date on Friday night, had not come home. This in itself was not unusual, according to his fraternity brothers.

But when he hadn't turned up the following afternoon, they'd called the cops.

And the police had found his empty car near the outskirts of town.

Foul play was suspected.

Demi's hands turned to ice.

"I don't believe it," she said, almost to herself.

"A friend of yours?" sneered Marge. Demi looked up to find Marge watching her closely, almost eagerly.

Like a predator waiting for the kill.

Forcing herself to appear calm, Demi picked up the chocolate and took a sip. She was pleased to see that her hands weren't shaking.

"Do you know him?" Demi answered the question with a question.

"Of course not," said Marge. "That fraternity is a little too — rich — for my blood." She wrinkled her nose, as if at a bad smell.

For once we agree on something, thought Demi. Aloud she said, "Yeah, well . . . thanks for the newspaper, Marge."

Marge stared at Demi a moment longer. Then the familiar sneer slipped back into place. "My pleasure," she said, and sauntered away.

Waiting until she was sure Marge was out of sight, Demi picked up the paper again. It rustled slightly in her hands. They'd begun to shake after all.

But she was able to read again, without too much difficulty, about the boy who'd disappeared.

Who'd disappeared after his date.

His last date.

With her.

Shake it off, she told herself. It's your job.

She got up, put her cup in the garbage can.

"Demi?"

Demi kept walking. Somehow, automatically, her steps had turned toward the *Chronicle* office. Kevin would know, a voice inside her said. He would know the story behind the news. And he wouldn't twist it up like Marge.

What did Marge know? *How much did Marge know?*

"Demi?"

At the bottom of the stairs, Demi turned. "Oh. Shannon."

"Where've you been all day?"

"Working," said Demi.

"At the library? I was there. I didn't see you." Shannon giggled. "Of course, I was kind of hanging out in the biology section."

"Why Shannon! How wicked," said Demi automatically. "Did you learn anything in the — biology — section?"

Shannon giggled. "You just have to know how to read a biology book. Or ask the cute guys there to help you."

"Any cute guy in particular?" asked Demi absentmindedly.

"Sure," said Shannon. She stopped giggling. "In fact, Jack was there for a little while. I'm surprised you didn't see him."

Jack.

"I haven't seen Jack in a while."

He said to tell you hello. I think he misses you, Demi."

"I don't miss him," said Demi.

"You're really through with Jack?"

"Really through," said Demi.

"I wonder if he's really through with you?" said Shannon softly.

Demi spun around. "What! What did you say!"

Surprised, Shannon stepped back. "What d'ya mean?"

"What did you just say? About Jack?"

"Just that I wondered if he was through with you. You know, if he's gotten over you. 'Cause he is awfully cute and if you . . ."

Demi relaxed. "You're interested? Be my guest."

"You're sure?" said Shannon.

"I'm sure," said Demi.

"Wow. Listen, I'm gonna go back to the dorm. Unless you want to hang out or anything."

"No. I've got more work to do. I'm on my way to the *Chronicle* office. Got to check out some news."

But Shannon didn't seem to be listening anymore. If she'd heard about Andrew, she hadn't made the connection.

Demi found that hard to believe. Maybe Shannon had, uncharacteristically, been at the library the whole day. Fear of midterms could do that to a person, even Shannon.

"I'll just head back to the dorm, then," Shannon was saying. "See you later?"

"Later," agreed Demi and watched Shannon bound happily across the grass.

Had Shannon had a thing for Jack all this time? wondered Demi. How did I not notice it?

Shaking her head, Demi made her way slowly to the *Chronicle* office.

"Call me," said the voice on the machine.

Why haven't the police been to see me yet? wondered Demi.

If they do come to see me, they're going to know. After all, I'm the last person to have seen three people before they were hurt.

Or kidnapped. Or killed.

Except the person who did it.

She'd missed the rest of the message. She rewound the tape, punched in the code for her ad in the personals, and played it again. The voice seemed familiar. But then, didn't every voice these days?

Stop that, Demi told herself again. She wrote down the number and folded the piece of paper into her pack.

If someone was doing this, the only way to find out *who* was to keep going out on dates.

Besides, she wasn't a quitter.

And she was beginning to get angry.

"I'll call you," she said aloud, softly. "Oh yes. I'll call you."

Chapter 11

The cops were waiting when she got to the Quad.

"Officer Chang. Officer DeVito. We've got to stop meeting like this," said Demi resignedly.

Neither of the officers smiled.

"You are here for me, aren't you?"

"What makes you say that?" asked Officer Chang.

"I read the paper," said Demi. She led the two officers to the same place in the reception area and sat down. "Shoot."

"According to our information," said Officer Chang, "You had a date with Andrew Decker Winston III?"

"Yes," said Demi.

"What happened."

We went to a Clint Eastwood movie. We went to dinner at a place called Nick's in the

Sticks. We went to shoot some pool. I forget the name of the place."

"Did you shoot pool?" asked Officer DeVito.

"No, I left," said Demi.

"Did you have a fight?"

"A disagreement."

The cop looked down at her notebook. "You entered the Q-Bar at approximately 11:45. You used the phone and waited by the door. You didn't talk to anyone. Approximately five minutes later, a cab picked you up. The cab brought you here."

"That's it," said Demi.

"And what was Andrew doing when you left him?"

"He left me," said Demi. "He drove away and left me in the parking lot."

Officer Chang made a careful note in her book. "I see."

Do you, thought Demi. But she knew better than to volunteer anything.

"Did anyone see you come home?"

"Yes," said Demi. "Friends. Shannon Thompson and Gigi LeFarge. We hung out for awhile, eating popcorn."

For a moment, Officer DeVito actually looked like she was going to smile. But the moment passed.

"Is there anything else you'd like to tell us?" asked Officer Chang.

Demi thought of the phone call. But she only said, "Like what?"

Officer DeVito closed her notebook. "Are you aware that you have had dates with two people recently? And that both people have been involved in accidents or suspicious incidents of some sort after their dates with you? And that you are the last person to have seen them before the events occurred?"

"Not the last person," said Demi.

"What do you mean?"

"The person who caused the — events — that would be the last person to have seen them."

The two officers exchanged glances.

"Wouldn't it?" Demi persisted.

She looked from one officer to the other. "Unless you think I'm the one who's doing this."

Instead of answering, the two officers stood up. "We'll be in touch," said Officer Chang. "Meanwhile, don't leave town without notifying us."

"Right," said Demi. She stood up, too. "Well, if you'll excuse me, I've got to go make a phone call."

Neither of the officers stopped her. But when

she was almost to the door, Officer Chang called out, "Ms. Blake!"

Demi turned.

"Any idea where Andrew is?"

Demi narrowed her eyes. "Your guess is as good as mine." She turned back around and walked out.

Getting ready for her date, Demi wondered vaguely where Shannon was. She'd made a point of being around when Demi got ready for her other CALL ME dates. With everything that had happened, Demi would have thought it was a sure bet Shannon would be here while she got ready for this one.

Hmmm.

Maybe she should enjoy the quiet while it lasted. After all, the fact that police officers had been to see Demi had not gone unnoticed in the dorm and Shannon had been the first to ask Demi about that. But then, Shannon had already known about Demi's date with Andrew.

"What are you going to *do*?" Shannon had cried dramatically, clasping her hands.

Demi had made herself look bored. "Do? Nothing. What can I do?"

Shannon had lowered her voice. "Do the police know?"

"Know what, Shannon?"

Undeterred by Demi's flat, forbidding tone of voice, Shannon had persisted. "About, you know, how those guys went out with you before they met their *doom*."

"Shannon, get with the program, okay? They didn't meet their doom. They had accidents. It was a coincidence. The cops don't even believe I had anything to do with it."

Shannon had looked puzzled and somehow, disappointed. "They don't? But . . ."

"Enough, Shan. If you want to know more, ask the cops."

Abruptly, Shannon's mood had changed. "Sorry, Demi. I didn't mean to be a ghoul. If there is anything I can do, you'll let me know, right?"

Demi had smiled at Shannon then, a real smile. Shannon might be irritating and indiscreet and gossip-hungry, but just when you thought you couldn't take it anymore, she turned into a warm, kind person. A friend.

A true friend. Someone she could trust. Confide in. If Shannon hadn't been there to listen, to take some of the heat of Demi's fear and frustration, who knows what would have happened by now?

The cops really would be coming after me, thought Demi wryly.

At least she could count on Shannon's friendship and support in this whole mess.

"I'm fine. But thanks."

"No problem," Shannon had answered gravely.

Shannon had known, but she'd been able to keep the secret so far. Surprisingly enough also, Demi's name had not been mentioned around campus in connection with Andrew's disappearance despite the fact that all his frat brothers had known he was going out with her. So Demi had been able to shrug off questions about the cops with a roll of her eyes and a murmur of a license mix-up.

So far.

I don't know how much more of this I can take, she thought.

But then, since when did she have a choice?

The phone rang and in spite of herself, Demi jumped. But it was only the voice of her date at the other end of the phone. "I'm here," he said. "Downstairs."

"I'll be right down," Demi said. The Quad, the dorm where many of the first year women at Salem lived, had a lot of old-fashioned rules. Among them was the rule that men weren't allowed in the dorms unannounced and unescorted. You had to go down and meet your dates.

Demi liked that. She liked making an entrance.

And in spite of all that had happened, she found herself looking forward to this date tonight. He had refused to give his name over the phone.

"It's a surprise," he'd insisted.

"Do I know you?" Demi had asked. For one uneasy moment, she'd wondered: was his voice the same as the threatening voice on the phone? But no, it couldn't be.

Somehow, she trusted the sound of his voice. Trusted him even before she'd met him.

Maybe this date would be a winner. Something to *not* write about in her article.

She checked her appearance in the mirror one last time: black jeans, a thin, oversized white lambswool sweater, her red-gold hair shining and loose around her face.

She was ready. She could handle anything.

Feeling confident and a little defiant Demi headed downstairs toward the Quad lobby. She pushed the doors open and walked into it.

He was standing there. Slowly he turned.

He took a step toward her.

"Demi," he said, softly.

"You!" she gasped. "It's you!"

Chapter 12

Brant walked slowly toward her, the smile on his face broadening.

"It *is* you," said Demi. "I thought I knew the voice on the phone.,"

"Glad to see me?" asked Brant.

Demi felt herself start to blush. She couldn't believe it. She never blushed. But the harder she tried to stop, the worse it got. She felt as if her whole body was blushing.

"Well?" said Brant.

With an effort, Demi got control of her wits.

"Of course," she said. "But now you know my darkest secret — I get dates out of the personals column in the school paper."

Brant reached out and took her hand. "So do I."

Smiling, Demi allowed Brant to lead her out of the dorm and into the early evening. The gloomy weather of the past week had receded, and a sort of early summer haze seemed to hang over the campus.

"Full moon coming soon," remarked Brant, gesturing toward the sky. They walked slowly across campus, in comfortable silence.

Finally Demi said, a laugh bubbling up in her throat, "Where are we going?"

"Going? Ah. We're going to have a good time." Brant pulled her closer, tucking her hand in his elbow. "Trust me."

And they did. It was as if all the other dates had been bad rehearsals. They went to a movie, and then to eat pizza. But no leering fraternity jocks waited in the entrance to the movie theater. No voice whispered unnecessary translations in her ear, or laughed raucously when someone shot someone up on the screen. No desperate hands clutched at her hands, no desperate words clutched at her heart.

It was fun. Demi had almost forgotten what fun could be. When Brant suggested they get the pizza and take it to the terrace of the Student Center overlooking the Commons instead of chowing in noisy Vinnie's, she agreed readily, without worrying about Brant's motivations. She was even able to forget the sense of forboding that had been haunting her.

Instinctively, intuitively, she trusted him.

Eating the pizza, laughing and talking, Demi

lost track of time and space. She was startled when the campus clock struck the three notes for three quarters after the hour.

"It's late!" she exclaimed in surprise. "It's a quarter to one!"

"I'm relieved to see you didn't turn into a pumpkin at midnight, Cinderella." Brant gathered up the pizza box and leftovers and dumped them in a nearby garbage can. When he came back, he sat down close to her.

Absurdly, Demi felt her heart begin to race, as if she were some sweaty-palmed kid on her first date.

She laughed softly.

"What?" said Brant, leaning closer.

She reached up and kissed him. Now she knew why her heart had been racing.

"That," she said.

"That I like," murmured Brant.

Once again she lost track of time. Only the slow, measured pace of footsteps brought her back to her senses. Suddenly, the feeling of being menaced, of being followed, of being threatened, all came back to her.

Who was watching her? Who was following her?

Was her kiss the kiss of death for Brant?

She pulled free abruptly, turning toward the sound.

Brant made an inarticulate sound of protest, leaning toward her, but she put her hand against his chest and held it there, feeling, subconsciously, the steady, reassuring thump of his heart.

"Who is it?" she called sharply. "Who's there?"

"Evening, kids," said a voice from the far shadows of the trees. A moment later, a figure in the navy uniform of campus security emerged and cut across the edge of the terrace away from the globe lights that edged the steps.

"Hey," said Brant, a thread of amusement in his voice.

"Oh," said Demi. "Hello."

The figure nodded and moved silently on, his footsteps as slow and relentless as doom.

"Relax," said Brant. He put his arms back around her and drew her head against his shoulder. He laughed softly. "Although I guess we probably shouldn't be out here so late. I'd better be getting you home, Cinderella."

"Yes," she said, reluctantly.

She felt his breath against her hair as he spoke. "I have a confession to make."

"Yes?"

"I knew it was you before I ever called the

dating service. I knew that was your advertisement."

Demi pulled back slightly to stare up at Brant. But his expression was masked by the semidarkness. "How? How did you know?"

Brant shook his head. "Oh, no. That's enough confession for one night. You'll have to wait for our next date to hear more."

He stood and reached out his hand. "C'mon, Cinderella."

She put her hand in his and smiled up at him trustingly. "Okay," she said. "When?"

"How about Friday night?" asked Brant as they cut across the campus back toward the dorm.

"Hmmm. Okay."

"I'll pick you up at eight. If the weather is still this good, wear picnic clothes."

"Picnic clothes."

"It'll be a full moon . . ." Brant leaned over and kissed her lightly.

"Doesn't the full moon bring out the lunatics?" asked Demi, matching her tone to his kiss.

"Oh. Right. I forgot *that* darkest secret of mine. But I'll do my best to behave."

Demi laughed softly. "Don't try *too* hard," she said.

Brant's hand tightened on hers.

"Is that a yes?" she teased.

He didn't answer.

"Brant?"

She looked up at him. But he wasn't looking down at her. He was looking past her, his eyes widening.

"Brant?"

He jerked her forward and gave her a push. "Get out of here!" he cried hoarsely. "Run!"

Chapter 13

Demi half-turned. Out of the corner of her eye she caught a glimpse of something white and eerie floating above the ground in the shadow of the trees.

Something hideous.

Something dead.

A sickening, sweet smell invaded her senses, making her head spin and her eyes water.

Brant spun her around and pushed her ahead of him. "Go!" he cried.

Panic swept over her. She obeyed mindlessly, blindly. She ran off the path into the dark, not knowing where she was going, not caring.

Then she remembered the security guard. Surely he was around somewhere?

She opened her mouth to scream.

And something clamped over it. She choked and fumes burned her throat.

"No," she tried to say but she couldn't speak.

And then she couldn't hear. Or feel.

Or do anything at all.

Dampness. The dank smell of decay.

Demi groaned. There was a sick, sweet smell in her mouth. Somehow it was familiar. For a moment, she flashed to the time she'd had her tonsils out when she was a little girl.

Her throat burned now as it had then. Her head ached.

But her tonsils were long gone. She wasn't a little girl anymore.

She groaned again and sat up.

Spidery fingers touched her face. With a cry she fell back, lashing out with her hand.

The branches of low bushes scraped her hand and arm.

She pulled her arm back and tried to see where she was. The dark world swung drunkenly in her vision. Distant lights whirled like the lights from a circus.

That would be one explanation for where I am, thought Demi giddily. I got sick on the merry-go-round.

She knew better, though. It wasn't that. Think. Think.

Remember.

Brant. His hand on hers. His face.

His face. The horror in his face.

And then she was running. She'd been about to scream for help when . . .

She groaned again and sat upright. The movement made her feel even sicker, but her head was clearing. She knew now what had happened to her. Someone had clamped a rag soaked in ether over her mouth.

How long had she been unconscious?

Where was she?

She pulled herself to her hands and knees and pushed forward through the low branches. A moment later, she squinted out past the last of them onto the Commons. She had been pulled or pushed into the low broad hedges that lined the terrace of the Student Center.

Dragging herself out of the hedges, she got shakily to her feet.

"Hello?" she called.

The darkness suddenly seemed to grow very still. To press in on her. She realized how alone she was. How very alone.

Stop it, Demi, she told herself. She put her cold hands to her face and rubbed her temples vigorously.

"Hello?" she called again defiantly.

A movement down on the Commons caught her eye. She turned toward it. What was happening down there in the dark?

And then it all came back to her: the terrible things that had happened to Lance and Phillip and Andrew.

And now to Brant.

NO!" she screamed, leaping forward. She stumbled, her legs shaky.

"NO!" she screamed again. "Help! Help me."

She ran forward into the dark. And then she saw it. Stretched out along the ground. It turned toward her. Blood trickled out of the corner of its mouth.

"Brant!" she screamed. "Brant!" and flung herself forward to save him.

Even as she fell, footsteps raced toward her. A moment later, a heavy hand gripped her shoulder and she was blinded by the beam of a flashlight.

"What is it? What's going on here?" asked a gruff voice.

In the light, Demi saw the campus security cop.

"What took you so long?" she cried.

The cop put a reassuring hand on her arm. "I was just coming up from my normal beat along the bottom of the Commons," he said, pointing away from the terrace.

"But I just saw you walk across the terrace!"

Keeping his hand on her arm, the cop

ignored her, leaning forward to speak a few quick words of command into his pager. Then he bent down on one knee beside Brant.

Brant's face was so pale, so pale. He didn't seem to be breathing.

Demi swayed dizzily. "Is he? Is he . . . ?"

"Can you hold this?" asked the cop. With an effort, Demi lifted the flashlight and kept it focused on Brant and the cop. With skillful, careful hands, the cop examined Brant. "He seems to be all right," he said after what seemed like an eternity. "Although I don't know what would have happened if you hadn't screamed for help like that. It looks like someone was serious about mugging this guy. Dead serious." The cop sniffed. "Much more of whatever they were knocking him out with, and he would have been a goner. You saved his life."

"I? I *saved* his life?" Demi started to laugh. She saw the cop's look of surprise and concern, read his expression of "the poor kid's hysterical" clearly, but she couldn't stop laughing.

Couldn't even stop laughing long enough to explain why she was laughing.

Because she knew she hadn't saved Brant's life. If anything, she'd almost killed him.

Because the price of a date with her looked like it was . . . death.

Chapter 14

The long night was over.

Demi was asleep.

She was sleeping the deep and dreamless sleep of exhaustion. She didn't move. She scarcely seemed to breathe.

Over in the student infirmary, Brant slept, too, a lock of dark hair across his pale forehead. His breath was even. He was unharmed. He could go home that afternoon, as soon as the doctor gave the okay.

In the hospital, Lance turned and muttered in his sleep. Even in his dreams, he hurt. His bones were still jarred, his body bruised from the collision with the car that had come out of nowhere to toss him in the air and let him come falling down to the unyielding pavement. Over and over in his dreams, he turned and watched the dark hulking mass come toward him. Felt himself freeze. Tried to get himself to run.

Over and over, he didn't move. Not until the impact. Not until he was flying high above the ground, knowing that when he fell, it would hurt worse than anything he'd ever imagined.

In another corridor in the same hospital, the police officer yawned and tilted back in his chair. Guard duty was a bore. And he, personally, didn't think anything was going to come of this. The detectives had been there a hundred times, and a hundred times come away empty. Whatever had happened to that Phillip kid was going to stay locked up in him. In his few lucid moments, he didn't remember. Didn't want to remember. Geez, who would want to remember someone trying to kill you?

Who would want to wake up and know that someone might be trying to kill you still?

Andrew didn't wake up at all. He never would again. He'd hit his head going down the side of the quarry. Slipped into the dank, dark water and rolled beneath an underwater overhang. He hadn't felt anything, except surprise when the hand with the evil-smelling cloth had snaked through his window at the traffic light. His last thought was that he wasn't letting any loser hitchhiker steal *his* car. . . .

They would find him soon.

But for the moment he floated quietly, quietly in his grave of water.

One person kept all the secrets.

One person knew all the answers.

A loner. A loser who was now a winner at the game.

Because the game was a game of life and death.

And that person was the only person who knew all the rules.

That person watched.

Laughed.

Cried.

But none of it was real.

The only thing that was real was the game.

The dating game.

The dying game.

Chapter 15

"Demi?"

Demi rolled on her stomach, pulled the pillow over her head. She only wanted to sleep. Why wouldn't they let her sleep?

"Demi?"

Giving up, Demi rolled back over.

"What?"

"Cranky," said Demi's roommate teasingly. She held out the phone. "It's for you. Someone named Brant. Want me to tell him to . . ."

"No!" Demi practically leaped from the bed. Ignoring her roommate's knowing grin, she said, "Brant! Brant, are you all right?"

"I'm fine. Just fine. I hear you may have saved my life."

"Oh, Brant," said Demi, not knowing whether to laugh or cry.

"So, just because I was dumb enough to get us mugged . . ."

"Mugged? But I saw this, this thing! You saw it too, Brant, I know you did."

Brant sighed. "I'm not sure what I saw, Demi. But I sure feel like I've been mugged. Anyway, you and I have told the cops everything we know. Let them worry about it.

"Now about our date on Friday night?" he continued.

"Friday night?"

"You've forgotten," said Brant mournfully. "Or is that a no?"

"No! I mean, *yes*. Oh, Brant, I don't know. I shouldn't . . ."

"Don't worry. It was just bad luck. I promise you, this doesn't usually happen until the *third* date." The laughter in his voice reassured Demi somehow. But how could she go out with him without telling him the truth?

And if she told him the truth, she'd have to tell him she'd started out on this dating thing for an article. Even if Brant meant more to her than research, could she convince him?

"Brant," she began.

"Say yes," he ordered.

She hesitated.

"Yes," he repeated. "Yes, Brant."

She took a deep breath. "Yes, Brant."

"Good," he said. "I'll pick you up at eight, don't be late."

"But are you okay?"

"I'll show you." His laugh was exuberant. "Trust me. I've never been better."

That day Demi pulled her ad from the paper.

Kevin nodded approvingly when she told him of her decision. "It's the right thing to do," he said.

"I don't know." Demi slid into the seat across from Kevin in the Caf. "I feel like a failure. A quitter."

"How many dates did you go out on?"

"Just four. Unless you count a second date with one of the guys on Friday night. You know him. Brant."

"Well, four might be enough for a feature. Do a little research on the history of dating, like that. And we don't have to run it right away. We could even save it for a special edition, like Valentine's Day."

"Next year?" protested Demi.

Kevin smiled at her. "It's okay. You'll have other assignments. Like here's one now: eat some of this sandwich. You look pretty wiped — like you could use some nourishment."

Demi looked down at the sandwich and realized she was ravenous. How long had it been since she'd eaten anything? The pizza on the terrace?

"Thanks," she said gratefully, and pulled the sandwich toward her.

"You know," said Kevin, "I admire your courage. And your perseverance."

"What're y'talking 'bout?" mumbled Demi around a mouthful of sandwich. She smiled to herself. There weren't many people she'd chow down in front of like she was doing with Kevin. He was so comfortable, so easy to be around.

Too bad he had such a witch like Marge for a girlfriend. Still, maybe he wasn't all that attached to Marge. Maybe he was waiting for something better to come along.

Demi tilted her head, studying him.

Kevin stopped talking. Smiled. Then asked, "What're you doing?"

"Thinking," said Demi.

"About me? I like that," said Kevin.

"About you, maybe," agreed Demi.

Kevin's eyes met hers. He took a deep breath. "Demi. Demi, I . . ."

"Aren't we a *cute* couple." True to form, Marge barged in with perfect bad timing.

"Marge," said Kevin unenthusiastically.

"Kevvvv," cooed Marge. She kissed him on the cheek and roughed up his hair. Like he was a little kid or a pet, thought Demi in disgust.

Kevin ducked his head from beneath her hand, and caught it in his.

Marge sat down and picked up the remains of Kevin's sandwich on his plate and took a big bite with big white teeth.

"My, what big teeth you have," said Demi, without thinking.

"What!" Marge spluttered. "What did you say?"

"Nothing. At least, nothing important," Demi answered hastily.

Marge narrowed her eyes. "I'm not the one who's the wolf, am I? I'm not the one people should be afraid of. You are, Miss Last Date Demi."

The sandwich turned to ashes in Demi's mouth. She put it down, swallowed, and said with difficulty, "What are you talking about, Marge?"

"Your little dating game," said Marge. "You think I'm stupid? You think I can't put two and two together? Every guy you've gone out with since you put that ad in CALL ME has met, shall we say, a bad end."

"What are you saying?"

Kevin interrupted Demi. "What are you talking about, Marge?"

Marge met his eyes defiantly. "I have my sources," she said. "Ms. Hot Date over here has had four dates. Four guys. Three have ended up in the hospital or infirmary. One is missing."

An angry flush crept up Kevin's cheeks. "How did you find that out?"

"C'mon Kevin. I read the police reports, okay. I see *her* name over and over. I know she's doing that jerk piece for the paper. It doesn't take a rocket scientist to figure it out."

"And it doesn't take a rocket scientist to figure out that it is something to be *kept quiet!*" Kevin shot back in a low, warning tone of voice.

Marge raised her eyebrows. "Really? What kind of journalism is that, Kevin? I'd call this a story. A really great story. Unless, of course, you have some reason for protecting little Demi here."

"Hey, wait a minute," said Demi.

"Reasons? I need reasons? I'm the managing editor," Kevin said.

"Does our fearless editor-in-chief know you're sitting on this? I bet she wouldn't like it." Marge pushed back from the table and stood up.

Demi sat, rooted in her seat with horror at Marge's maliciousness.

But Kevin caught Marge's hand. "Marge."

Marge looked down at Kevin, then pulled him up to stand beside her. Close beside her. "What?"

"The cops want this kept quiet for a little longer," Kevin told her. "They're conducting an investigation, remember? And we want to stay on good terms with the cops, don't we?"

Marge studied Kevin for a moment from beneath her lashes. Then she smiled. "They're not the only ones we want to stay on good terms with, are they, Kevin?"

Kevin looked back at Marge. He didn't answer.

But something in his expression must have been answer enough for Marge.

"See you later, Demi-date," said Marge. She turned and began to walk away, still holding Kevin's hand.

"Later," Kevin managed, as he allowed himself to be pulled after her.

Stunned, shaken, Demi watched them walk away. "Talk about the date from hell," she muttered.

Witch was too good a word for Marge, she decided. Kevin deserved someone better. Much, much better. It was more than time that someone put a stop to Marge.

Or maybe she had it backwards. Maybe it was Marge who was trying to put a stop to her. . . .

Chapter 16

"So is this one of *those* dates?" asked Shannon.

It was the old familiar scenario. Demi was getting ready for her date with Brant. Shannon was sprawled across Demi's bed, Gigi sitting on the floor propped against it.

"No," said Demi.

"Really?" said Shannon.

"Really," said Demi.

"It is serious, then, this date?" asked Gigi.

"It's just our second date. Good grief." Demi was annoyed.

Gigi shrugged, undeterred by Demi's emotion. "Sometimes, one date is enough." She paused, then added thoughtfully, "Often, one date is more than enough!"

Demi rolled her eyes. "You can say that again."

With one fluid, catlike motion, Gigi stood up. "Okay. Me, I have a date also. A study date.

He is smart. In math. I do not like math."

Shannon put her hand dramatically over her heart. "Gigi! You only like him for his *mind*."

Gigi shrugged again. "No. Just for his math." She walked out of the room, leaving Shannon and Demi in hysterics.

"God, that Gigi, she is so *cold* sometimes. I wish I could be like that," gasped Shannon at last.

"You could *never* be like that," said Demi.

Shannon tilted her head. "You don't think so?"

"I know so. You're too — too kind and friendly. Besides, Gigi's style wouldn't suit you at all."

Sighing, Shannon said, "Yeah, I guess you're right." She looked at Demi. "So, are you okay? Feeling okay and all, I mean."

Demi made a movement as if to brush the subject away. "I'm fine."

Shannon refused to be put off. "Demi. Do you think it's wise? To go out like this? I mean, until the cops figure out what is going on?"

Demi had asked herself the same question a thousand times. But she couldn't be sure if there was a right answer. She said now, "Listen, I don't know what's going on. Maybe nothing. Maybe it really is all a coincidence. But whatever it is, I'm not going to hide in my room."

Shannon stood up. "You're sure? You're absolutely going out on this date?"

"I'm sure," said Demi, staring defiantly at her friend.

"Then — have a great time." Shannon gave Demi a brilliant, wicked grin, and strolled out of the room after Gigi.

Demi pulled on a jacket. Checked herself out in the mirror. Yes. Dressed for success at a picnic. Especially this picnic.

She was just walking out the door when the phone rang. Smiling, she picked it up. "I'll be right down," she almost sang.

But it wasn't Brant.

"What's going to happen on *this* date?" the voice whispered.

"Who are you!" Demi screamed. "Tell me who you are so I can kill you!" Her hands were shaking. Rage flooded her body.

But the whispering voice remained calm.

"Ooooh," it breathed. "Kill me. I like that. . . . little Demi does Death. Sweet Demi, pretty Demi.

"Dead Demiiiii . . ."

The phone went dead.

Demi slammed down the receiver and

doubled over. She felt as if she'd been punched in the stomach. What was she going to do?

"I won't give up," she whispered. "I won't give up. I'll fight you. I'll win!"

The phone rang again.

She grabbed it. Waited.

This time the voice was welcome and familiar. "Demi?"

"Brant." Demi took a deep breath. Smiled. Made the smile come into her voice. "Brant. I'll be right down."

"*Vroom, vroom*," said Brant, gesturing.

Demi started to laugh. "It's a — car?"

"Beauty is in the eye of the beholder," said Brant, pretending to be hurt.

"It's a *beautiful* car," said Demi, struggling to keep a straight face. "Is it yours?"

"It's a sort of a group investment," explained Brant. "No, no, no, the door's broken. You climb *over* it. That's where the convertible top comes in handy."

Demi swung over the top of the door and slid into the seat, smiling. She was beginning to expect the unexpected with Brant. And she couldn't help but compare this car to the sleek car that Andrew had driven. This one had doors that were different colors, strange dents and dings, and a convertible top that was tied back like a manic accordian. The car also, she discovered as Brant slid in beside her and cranked it up, made a noise like a tank.

And she liked it much, much better than Andrew's car. But then, she liked Brant much, much better than Andrew.

Much better, in fact, than anyone she'd ever met.

Careful Demi, she warned herself. Don't lose your perspective on this guy. You hardly know him.

But she felt like she knew him. She felt as if she'd known him forever.

They drove, as she had driven with Andrew, through the town and out through the suburbs. Soon they were in the wooded, rolling hills and neat farmlands that surrounded the town. The full moon had begun to rise, and the world looked like a shadow box of silver and black.

Demi leaned her head back against the worn vinyl seat and took a deep breath. The air tasted good, different somehow from the air of town. She looked out at the silvered fields of old corn stalks standing sentry next to the freshly plowed new fields, furrowed as if by enormous gophers.

She smiled and turned toward Brant, watching him drive, watching his sure hands on the wheel. As if he felt her gaze, Brant glanced toward her and smiled.

"We're almost there!" he shouted.

She nodded.

A minute later, they turned down a slight hill onto a rutted dirt road. The car lurched through the tunnel of trees and emerged soon after at a wide, sandy parking area. Brant pulled to one side of the parking lot and turned off the engine.

The silence after the roar of the engine seemed huge, overwhelming. For a moment, the silence continued. Then, tentatively, the early frogs picked up their chorus. Far off, Demi heard the call of a pair of mourning doves, testing the night.

Brant reached beneath the seat and handed Demi a flashlight. "I don't think we'll be needing this, but you never can tell," he said. He reached in the backseat and pulled out a basket and what looked like an enormous lunch box. Getting out of the car, he set them on the hood, then walked around and lifted Demi over the edge of the door as she was climbing out of the car.

She slid easily down into his arms and just as easily and naturally lifted her face for a kiss.

When she pulled away, she was smiling.

"I like picnics," she declared.

"And we haven't even gotten started," Brant replied, returning her smile. "We're about to have a picnic at historic Bottomless Lake."

He reached over and handed her the lunch box and then took her hand and led the way down a narrow path.

He was right. They didn't need the flashlight. In the bright light of the full moon, Demi could see every detail of the path and much of the woods around them. Once Brant stopped her, squeezing her hand. But this time, it wasn't something coming to get them, but a racoon who had stopped on the path ahead of them. It regarded them calmly for a moment, then turned and sauntered away.

"Wow," breathed Demi.

They continued on and at last emerged from the woods.

They were at the edge of a lake, a vast, silver sheet of water beneath the silver sky, broken by a pier that stretched out a long way across the surface.

This time, Demi couldn't think of anything to say. She just stared and stared. Then she turned and hugged Brant, hard.

"Hey," said Brant. "I'm supposed to be the lunatic. Welcome to Bottomless Lake."

They walked out onto the dock and spread their picnic at the end. It was a feast. Demi would always remember that. A feast, but she couldn't remember what it was. Only the laughter, and the comfortable silences and the swell of the water beneath the pier in the light breeze and the benign silver cloak of the moon thrown over them.

This time, it wasn't the chime of a clock that brought her back to reality, but Brant, propped against a tall piling on the dock, his arm around her shoulder.

"Late," he murmured into her ear. She turned her head and said, "Mmmm?"

"Continuing late until morning," said Brant. "Which it will be if we don't leave soon."

"I don't want to leave," said Demi. "I wish I could stay like this forever."

"Me, too," said Brant. His arms tightened around her, then loosened. "Does this mean you want to go out again sometime?"

"Tomorrow?" asked Demi.

She heard the rumble of his laugh in his chest beneath his flannel shirt. "I accept," he said.

They stood up slowly, and in dreamy quiet began to gather up the remains of the picnic. In silence, they carried everything up the path to the car.

"The flashlight," exclaimed Demi as she was about to climb into the car.

"No problem." Brant leaned forward and kissed Demi. "Wait here."

"I will," said Demi. She leaned back against the car and stared up at the sky. The moon had begun to set. She heard the raucous cry of a faraway bird. Strange how sound traveled in the woods. And across the water. Probably if she called Brant right now, softly, he would hear her, all the way down at the lake.

How did animals hunt when sound carried so easily? How were they able to walk silently across the leaves and through the underbrush? It seemed impossible, and yet it must be so.

Human hunters, too, must be able to do the same thing.

The thought caught in her brain.

Human hunters.

No, of course, she was just letting her imagination get away from her. The only hunters in these woods were foxes and racoons and hawks. Animal predators.

No human ones.

But wasn't Brant taking an awfully long time to come back from the lake?

Chapter 17

Demi stirred restlessly. The moon had gotten perceptibly lower. Soon she wouldn't be able to see by its light. Soon it would be that darkest time of night, the darkness before the dawn.

Brant had been gone a long, long time. Too long.

Maybe he'd fallen. Or maybe he just couldn't find the flashlight.

That was probably it.

She'd give him five more minutes and then go help him look.

The minutes passed like hours. She found herself straining to hear the sound of his footsteps on the path, thinking every flash of silver moonlight on a wind-twisted leaf was the beam of the flashlight coming toward her.

But five minutes passed, and no Brant.

Resolutely, Demi pushed herself away from the car and started down the path.

* * *

The dock stretched out onto the silver-toned water, a dark division in the light.

"Brant?" called Demi softly.

As softly as she called, her voice traveled out over the water.

But no one answered.

"Brant?" she called again, less tentatively, more loudly.

The echo of her voice came back from a near shore of the lake.

It was the only thing that answered her.

Except a faint rustling of the underbrush on the trail behind her.

She whirled around. "Brant? Brant, is that you?"

No one answered. The woods grew still again.

Her heart began to pound heavily, painfully. She turned back toward the dock and stepped out on it. "Brant?" she called. "Brant?"

She walked into the answerless darkness, treading as quietly as she could on the old boards, trying to hear every sound the night made.

Trying to hear Brant.

But Brant didn't reply to her calls.

She reached the end of the dock. The lake stretched before her, darker now. Bottomless darkness. The moon was almost gone. The light was disappearing.

Panic welled up in her, choking her, making her sweat the acrid sweat of fear.

Stop it.

And then she saw it. A faint ripple in the sheet of water. A stirring, like the feeble thrashing of hands, trying to break the surface, trying to grasp the air.

"Brant!"

It was a hand.

"Brant!"

Demi leaped forward. Reached the edge of the dock.

The blow that hit the back of her head made her see stars. Stars as beautiful and bright as the moon. Somehow, instinctively sensing a second blow, she ducked. This time, whatever it was hit her on the shoulder.

She lost her balance and fell into the icy dark water of Bottomless Lake.

Chapter 18

The water was colder than ice. Colder than death.

The stars exploded behind her eyes. They grew and grew, blinding her. A tunnel of stars.

All she had to do was follow the stars. Then she'd be safe. Warm.

That was it. Death wasn't cold at all.

It was warm. It was warm if you just stopped fighting. Stopped caring.

She spread out her arms.

The movement made her whole body jerk with pain and cold and shock.

The shock of still being alive.

Life.

Death.

She hung there in the bitter-cold darkness for a moment longer.

Then she kicked toward the star-exploding surface of the water.

Her clothes pulled on her like malevolent hands, the malevolent hands of children begging her to stay, stay here, stay here in the drowning cold with us.

But she struggled doggedly upward. The edges of the stars exploding in her head turned into sharp knives, cutting her brain. The more she struggled the more they slashed and cut and hurt.

Hurt.

Hurt.

Her lungs hurt. She couldn't breathe.

To fight so hard and to have death win after all.

"No!" she cried, and icy water rushed into her mouth.

Icy water.

Then air.

She broke the surface of the water, thrashing, floundering.

And felt rather than saw the blow come down toward her, the dark massive weight of something heavy and crushing.

Killing.

She dove again, although every fiber of her being wanted to stay above the water.

To breathe.

She turned blindly in the water, a clumsy lost human, trying to divine which way was out toward the center of the lake and away from the hunter.

Turned and felt something brush against her in the frozen wet dark. A hand.

A drowned hand?

Brant?

She reached out, dreading what she would feel.

Nothing.

But maybe it was a sign. She swam in the direction of the ghostly frozen hand that might- or might not have touched her. Swam and swam. Swam forever in dragging, drowning waters.

Until at last she had to come up for air again.

She broke the surface this time and saw — nothing.

The moon had set.

Awkwardly, painfully, she began to tread water, trying not to splash, wondering how far the tell-tale ripples would spread, wondering if her ragged breath was as loud as it sounded in her ears.

Then she heard it. A voice.

Distorted. Muffled.

Whispering her name.

"Demiiiii."

"Demiiiiiiiii."

Chapter 19

How long had she been there? Her arms were numb. Her whole body ached with cold and exhaustion. She moved them feebly, barely keeping her chin above the water. Reaching down, she struggled free of her boots and socks. The weight of them fell away and it helped. Her chin lifted marginally above the water.

Was the darkness growing less?

She thought it was. But whether that was good or bad, she could no longer tell. The light would tell her where the shore was.

But it would also tell the hunter, if he was still there, where to find his prey.

Yes. A faint dim light was beginning to touch the sky. East was that way.

But which way was death?

* * *

"Demi."

She heard it clearly this time.

"Brant?" she whispered. She turned toward the sound.

And then she saw it. A beam of light. And then another. Flashlights, crisscrossing the darkness not so far away.

"Hello!" a voice called.

"Demi?" another voice called. "Demi, are you all right?"

Footsteps sounded blessedly, solidly, reassuringly on the dock.

"Demi?" another, unfamiliar voice called.

"Here! I'm over here!" she choked on a mouthful of water, kicked upward. "Here!" she called.

The lights flashed out across the water.

With a mighty effort she raised her hand and waved. "Here! I'm here. It's me. It's me. . . ."

With her last strength, she began to swim toward the lights.

Although it was probably only minutes, it seemed like hours before she got close to the dock. Light danced across the water. Missed her. Then she was swimming into the beam of a flashlight.

"Oh my God," a voice said.

Hands reached down and lifted her up. She felt as if her arms were being yanked from the sockets, as if the lake was quicksand, sucking and pulling her back down.

With a last mighty heave she was pulled up onto the dock.

She had won.

She was alive.

Chapter 20

"What happened?" someone said.

"Don't try to talk," someone else said. Hands pulled roughly at her clothes. A woman's voice said, "Here," and her wet clothes were peeled away and warm clothes and a blanket wrapped around her. She was being lifted, carried, off the dock, through the woods. Blue lights flashed across her vision and she heard the staccato of a police radio.

"Are you all right? Demi?" a voice said urgently in her ear.

"Brant?" she muttered.

A momentary silence met her question, then the voice said, "Where's Brant?"

"Brant," she repeated hoarsely. She turned and with blurring vision, saw Kevin.

"Kevin," she whispered. And then she knew no more.

* * *

The lights hurt her eyes. She closed her eyes. Someone whimpered protestingly. She opened her eyes again, cautiously, turned her head. The lights weren't the jagged edges of the stars. They were the lights of a pale, white room.

"Demi?"

Carefully she focused. "Kevin."

He picked up her hand. Her fingers closed convulsively around his. "Oh, Kevin. How did you find me?"

Kevin, looking pale and frightened, and for the first time since she'd known him, not the news reporter in control, smiled sheepishly.

"It was — I don't know — it was a feeling I had. You'd told me about your date, remember? In the Caf yesterday. I — I called Shannon. She said you hadn't come back. So I kind of tracked you down."

"How?"

"Brant's friends. They all own that car of his together. He'd told them where he was going, so when you didn't come back, I — I kind of took matters into my own hands. I'm sorry. I hope you don't think I — "

"You saved my life." To her horror, tears welled up in Demi's eyes. She turned her head away so he couldn't see, blinking rapidly. When she'd gotten control of herself again, she turned back to Kevin.

"Brant," she whispered.

Now it was Kevin's turn to look away. He bit his lip.

"Kevin? Where's Brant? Look at me!"

Slowly Kevin met her eyes. Before he even shook his head, she knew the answer.

"It's not true," she said. "It can't be true."

"Oh, Demi, I'm sorry. They looked everywhere. There's no sign of him. They're still searching, but they don't hold out much hope."

"Bottomless Lake," she said.

"It's happened there before," Kevin said.

"Not this time," she said. "He's not dead, I know he's not dead."

Kevin's fingers tightened on hers. He didn't answer.

The days that followed were worse than any nightmare that Demi could ever imagine. When they at last let her out of the hospital, away from the poking and prying of the doctors and the police, she crept back to her room and shut herself away from everyone. Away from the curious stares and the curious questions disguised as sympathetic inquiries. Away from the speculation and the talk. Away from the rumors.

Away from everything but her own grief.

If it hadn't been for Kevin, she might have gone mad.

But she didn't. And one day, when the sun was shining and the leaves were unfurling on the trees, she got dressed and went out into the world again.

Kevin was waiting for her. Leaning on his arm like an invalid, she made her way slowly across campus.

She'd gotten her wish. People knew who she was. They pointed at her and stared at her. They knew her name.

She endured it. Endured Jack's smug kindness. Endured Shannon's eager help. Endured the flat speculation in Gigi's eyes. Endured the furtive triumph she met in Marge.

She endured it all because she couldn't feel anything. Nothing at all.

Except when the nightmares came. She could feel those. The hand reaching out to her in the darkness. A hand of flesh, but the flesh peeling away so that it was the bones that clutched her.

A voice calling her from the other side of midnight, from the end of time.

Demiiii.

Help me.

Save meeeeee.

She never answered.

She always woke up.

But the nightmare never ended.

"Demi?"

"Hmmm?"

"Have you been listening to me?"

"You want to send a reporter to the state convention this year and . . ."

"And it could be you. What do you think?"

With a great effort of will, Demi focused on Kevin.

They were sitting in the Campus Grill. Odd, she thought idly, that it would be called the Campus Grill. People from Salem hardly ever came there.

She was glad of that. It was becoming her favorite place.

She lifted her coffee cup and drained it and signaled to the waitress for more.

"Me?"

"Demi, get with the program. Wake up. You can't go on like this forever!"

"I can't?"

"No!" Kevin slammed his hand down on the table so hard that his coffee sloshed over the rim of his cup. "No!

"Okay," said Demi agreeably. Easier to agree than to argue. To point out that she *could* go on like this forever. That Brant was dead and it was her fault. That somehow, some way, she had caused injury and death and destruction to everyone she'd gone out with.

"Demi, look at me. You're alive. Alive. It's not your fault. What happened, happened. But it's over."

"Okay."

"Demi, people care about you. I — I care about you."

Demi blinked. Kevin seemed so far away. Everybody did. "Okay."

Kevin leaned closer. "Demi, I really care about you. I know how you felt about Brant — "

"Do you?"

" — but you can't stop living because of that. Listen, this Friday, why don't I take you out? On a real date."

"Careful, Kevin. A date with me could be fatal."

"I'm serious! Demi, listen to me."

For a moment she focused. Saw Kevin. Saw the hurt and concern in his eyes. And something more.

She looked away from the intensity she saw there. The caring. She didn't want it. Didn't need it.

"I can't Kevin. I'm sorry."

"Demi — "

She shook her head. Stumbled to her feet. "No! No! If you want a date, put an ad in CALL ME. But just leave me alone, do you hear? LEAVE ME ALONE."

She ran. Ran without looking back. Ran back to her room and her nightmares. Ran back to wait for it to be over.

Whatever it was.

Chapter 21

When the call came, she wasn't even surprised. She'd been lying in her room in the early evening dusk, watching the shadows lengthen on the ceiling.

She'd been so intent on thinking about nothing at all that she didn't even hear the phone ring at first. Then she ignored it.

But it kept on ringing.

At last she got up and answered it.

"Hello?"

"I'm that kind of guy. Are you my kind of girl? Let's make a date for a night you'll never forget. . . ."

"Who is this?" she whispered.

"You'll see."

"No," she whispered even more softly.

"Yes," mocked the voice.

It was a voice she'd heard before. In her dreams. Or in her nightmares.

"Who are you?" she asked.

"Your date, Demi. Will you be mine?"

"I won't. I won't!"

"I think you will. You have a weakness for the truth."

"I won't. . . ."

"The clock tower. Half past midnight tonight."

The line went dead.

136

Chapter 22

The clock began the double toll that marked the half hours. Day is done, thought Demi.

She stepped out of the shadow of the trees and walked toward the tower.

The door to the tower stairs opened easily beneath her hand. She walked across the uneven stone floor and looked up. At first, she could see nothing. Then her eyes got used to the dark and she realized that some light was coming through the windows that lined the stairs. Enough light to see.

And be seen.

She felt the reassuring weight of the flashlight, a heavy, old flashlight made of stainless steel and heavy as a hammer, in her jacket pocket.

But she didn't take it out.

Instead she began to climb the stairs.

It was a dizzying ascent up, up the curved,

shallow steps, worn in the middle. The low railing on the outside seemed to float in the darkness, hardly enough to keep a body from falling.

She wouldn't think about that. She climbed on.

At last she reached the top. The door at the top of the stairs was an old one, made of heavy wood and cast iron, like something in a medieval fortress. But it opened, too, quietly, like a door in a twisted fairy tale.

She wouldn't have been surprised to meet a Rapunzel on the other side, spinning gold to straw.

No one turned to meet her. The bell hung high above, still and silent. All around, the stone arches opened to views across the campus and out to the town and the world beyond.

She walked to the center of the tower and turned.

And saw Kevin standing there.

She frowned. "Kevin?"

"Demi."

"But it couldn't have been you! I would have recognized your voice."

Now Kevin frowned. "Me? What are you talking about, Demi?"

"What are you doing here?"

Still frowning, Kevin took a step forward.

"What I've been doing all along. Keeping an eye on you. Taking care of you."

The layer of darkness that had weighed upon her like a smothering quilt lifted slightly. "Taking care of me? I don't need taking care of."

"Demi, look at you. What are you doing now? Is it sane? Is it taking care of yourself?"

As if she were a sleepwalker coming out of a long, long dream, Demi looked around. What was she doing there?

Kevin was right. It was crazy.

"A date," she said aloud. "He called me for a date."

"Who called you, Demi? That voice you've been hearing? You're not well. No one could be, if they'd been through what you've been through."

Another layer of darkness slid away. Demi shook her head as if she were trying to clear it. "I know what I heard. That's why I'm here."

"Demi." Kevin took another step toward.

Demi slid her hand into her pocket, let her fingers slide along the smooth metal of the old flashlight.

"Kevin," she answered.

Kevin paused. "You do trust me, don't you? I saved your life."

"You did," she agreed.

She looked at Kevin, so safe, so familiar.

"Someone has been after you, Demi. This much I know. But you can't keep taking chances like this. Let the police do the work . . . but then, you didn't call the police, did you?"

She shook her head. Frowning. Confused. "Kevin," she whispered.

Then she looked past Kevin. And her eyes widened when she realized who she saw.

Chapter 23

"Brant!" cried Demi, "Oh, Brant. You're alive! I knew you weren't dead. I knew it!"

"Demi," said Brant. His voice was familiar. Comforting.

She took a step toward him.

"Demi, stop!" Kevin cried out.

Demi turned halfway toward Kevin. "It's Brant! Don't you see, Kevin? He can tell us what happened!"

Kevin shook his head. "Demi, think! Brant can tell you what happened — *yes*. Because he *is* what happened. Can't you see that this is all a setup? That it's Brant who's been stalking you? Brant who's been trying to kill you?"

"What are you talking about?"

"Brant's known about the CALL ME article from the beginning. He was waiting to meet me at the newspaper offices the day we had the meeting about it. He heard the whole thing."

Demi's eyes widened. It was true. It had to be true. She remembered Brant's "confession." How else could he have known?

"Brant," she said dully, feeling sick.

"Don't listen to him, Demi! It's true, I did overhear you planning to put the ad in and do the article, but . . ."

"And then he figured out how to pick up the messages. It was easy, hanging around me, hanging around the office. He knew your every move. He tracked you, followed you, watched you."

"It's not true!" Brant cried. "It wasn't me. It was you, Kevin. *You!* You're the one who knew everything Demi was doing. You're the one who is obsessed with her. You're the one who has been stalking every guy she's gone out with!"

Demi looked from Kevin to Brant.

"Don't trust him," said Kevin. "He's a pathological liar. You want to believe him, Demi, I know you do. But you can't!"

"You must trust me," said Brant. "I suspected Kevin, but I wasn't sure. I went to the police. They didn't believe me, so I set up the date at the lake. I thought that would be sure to make Kevin give himself away, to prove it."

"You used me?" asked Demi. "You used me as *bait?*"

"No. No, it wasn't like that."

The last layer of darkness lifted. Demi turned to face Brant, rage burning away the dull stupor in which she'd been living . . . "You *used* me! How could you? You let me think you were dead!"

"To protect himself, Demi. Don't you see." Kevin stepped forward, his voice urgent, his face pale. "That's the kind of person he is. He's protecting himself still. If you believe his lies, if you trust him now, we're both going to die."

"Who called me tonight?" demanded Demi. "Which one of you called me?"

"Kevin," answered Brant.

"Brant," said Kevin at the same time.

Above her, she heard, vaguely, the whir and click of levers and pulleys and motors. The clock tower was getting ready to chime.

"Demi," said Brant.

"Demi, no. Look at *me*," cried Kevin.

With a great, grinding groan, the mechanism began to pull the heavy iron bell clapper back.

"We've got to get out of here," cried Brant. "Demi!"

"Demi!" screamed Kevin. He reached toward her. From the other side, she sensed, rather than saw Brant move.

She froze for a moment, like an animal trapped in headlights.

Then she leaped forward, and with the supernatural strength of terror, pulled open the heavy door to the stairs and began to run for her life.

Hands caught her. She jerked free.

She was through the door. Her feet slipped on the shallow stone stairs. She grabbed the railing and hung over it for a dizzying, sickening moment.

Something crashed into her. She turned, clinging to the railing and saw Kevin and Brant just behind her at the top of the stairs. They were locked in a mortal embrace, Kevin's hands around Brant's throat.

"Demi," gasped Brant. "Help me. Demiii."

It was the voice from the lake.

With a great shudder the bell in the tower began to ring.

The noise was deafening. Staggering, Demi stumbled over to the door and threw her weight against it, slamming it shut.

"Aaaaaaah," she screamed, stumbling, falling down the stairs.

For a moment, Kevin loosened his grip. The three of them collided. Hands tore at Demi. Once again she jerked free as the bell began to toll.

Brant and Kevin tumbled past her. Down, down, down they rolled.

Trembling, struggling to keep her senses, Demi went after them.

Kevin had Brant from behind now, pulling his head back, back. She saw the agonized expression on his face.

"Demmmi," he croaked.

She saw the expression on Kevin's face.

Her hand closed around the heavy metal shaft of the old flashlight. She pulled it from her pocket.

As the bell tolled for the final time, she raised the flashlight and brought it down.

Again.

And again.

And again.

Chapter 24

"Demi?"

"Go away," she answered. "I'm being sick."

"Not surprising," said the voice. Officer Chang's face appeared around the door. "You'll be pleased to know, I'm sure, that Kevin will be all right. You only gave him a concussion."

"Only?"

"He's in custody. He'll be in the hospital tonight for observation. You don't have anything else to worry about."

"Thanks a lot," muttered Demi.

Officer Chang's face broke into a smile. "Anytime," she said. "Oh, by the way, there's someone waiting to take you home."

"Maybe I won't be sick after all," said Demi.

A few minutes later, she emerged from the cubicle in the station house to find Brant waiting on one of the orange plastic chairs outside the door.

"Aren't you supposed to be dead?" she asked, brushing past him.

"You saved my life. Again," said Brant.

"It wasn't you, specifically, I was saving."

"I see." Brant fell into step beside her. "Well, can I give you a ride home as a thank-you anyway?"

Demi glared at him. Why did he have to be so cute? And charming?

"You used me," she said, but she knew she didn't sound as angry as she had before.

"You used me," said Brant. "You were just dating me for that article you were doing."

"I was not. I mean, well . . ." Demi's voice trailed off. Hastily, she said, "So what's the whole story here? Kevin did it all?"

"He was obsessed with you. When you weren't interested, he went over the edge. Then when you started this dating thing, he saw it as a perfect opportunity to warn people off and to make himself a hero, indispensable to you. The only problem was, you weren't falling for it. You were just too tough. Too independent."

"Flattery helps," said Demi. They'd reached

the car. Without looking at Brant she swung over the door and into the seat.

Brant slid into the other side.

"Then I came along. And Kevin decided I was a real threat. He was following us that night, disguised as a campus security guy. He did that a lot. No one even noticed him. All they saw was the uniform.

"He listened to us. Watched us. He'd already sensed this might be more than just a dating game and he'd stashed a sheet he treated with some kind of glow-in-the-dark stuff in a nearby hollow tree, along with some ether."

Demi made a face, remembering the sickening, sweet smell of the ether.

Brant went on. "Hearing us talk, he kind of lost it. He decided I had to die immediately. And maybe he wanted to scare you a little more.

"Only he didn't know I had an idea about what was going on. That's what saved my life that night at Bottomless Lake. I sensed him and he didn't quite knock me out. I was able to stay afloat and get out of range. But I wasn't able to warn you in time."

"Was that you calling me? After I went in?"

"Not at first. That was Kevin. I think he'd decided to kill you and me. If he couldn't have you, nobody could. But at the very end, it was me. I figured he'd gone. Then he came back with the police. And I made myself scarce . . ."

"And Lance and Phillip and Andrew?"

"Kevin. Hit and run for Lance — he's just lucky he's still alive. Phillip he hit on the head and then tried to make it look like a suicide. But Phillip survived, too."

"Not Andrew, though." Demi forgot her anger at Brant, remembering the police officer's face as he old them what they'd found that very day in the old quarry.

"There were fingerprints on Andrew's belt. Kevin didn't think about that."

"Poor Andrew. If only I'd . . ."

"Kevin is sick, Demi. It's not your fault. If it hadn't been you, it would have been someone — or something — else that set him off."

"But Kevin seemed like such a nice, normal, quiet guy."

Brant turned the car back toward campus. "Yeah. Well, normal. What's normal got to do with it?"

They rode in silence until they reached the dorm.

"So, what now?" asked Brant, pulling to a stop outside her dorm.

Demi looked toward him. Looked away. Then she smiled, a little smile.

Brant saw it. She could tell by the tone of

his voice as he leaned toward her.

"Demi?"

"Hmmm?"

"Want to go out with me some time?"

She smiled as she reached up to kiss him.

"Call me," she whispered.

Return to Nightmare Hall

. . . if you dare.

The voice on the telephone was unrecognizable.

It was only a whisper. But not the soft, sweet whisper of a person in love. Not the soothing, comforting whisper of one friend to another. Not the conspiratorial, sly whisper of someone passing on gossip. Nothing so harmless as any of those.

This whisper was sinister, chilling, the voice low and threatening. It wafted through the wires like poisonous air, slithering out on Shea's end in a dark, sickening cloud, enveloping her in dread.

Becuse she had brought this on herself. And now she didn't know how to stop it.

This call was only the beginning, she knew that.

There would be others.

The whispers would continue.

About the Author

"Writing tales of horror makes it hard to convince people that I'm a nice, gentle person," says **Diane Hoh**.

"So what's a nice woman like me doing scaring people?

"Discovering the fearful side of life: what makes the heart pound, the adrenaline flow, the breath catch in the throat. And hoping always that the reader is having a frightfully good time, too."

Diane Hoh grew up in Warren, Pennsylvania. Since then, she has lived in New York, Colorado, and North Carolina, before settling in Austin, Texas. "Reading and writing take up most of my life," says Hoh, "along with family, music, and gardening." Her other horror novels include *Funhouse*, *the Accident*, *The Invitation*, *The Fever*, and *The Train*.